BLACK WINGS HAS MY ANGEL

BLACK WINGS HAS MY ANGEL

D0207255

BLACK WINGS HAS MY ANGEL

ELLIOTT CHAZE

Bruin Books
The Emerald Empire
Eugene, Oregon

Published by
Bruin Books, LLC
June, 2011

First Published in the United States by
Gold Medal Books in 1953

This book was designed and edited by Jonathan Eeds
Graphics design by Michelle Policicchio

Printed in the United States of America
ISBN 978-09826339-7-7
Bruin Books, LLC
Eugene, Oregon, USA

Visit the scene of the crime at www.bruinbookstore.com

For Jane Grigsby,
an absolute champion

Part I

Chapter One

I'D BEEN ROUGHNECKING on a drilling rig in the Atchafalaya River for better than sixteen weeks, racking the big silver stems of pipe, lugging the sacks of drilling mud from barge to shore, working with my back and guts and letting my mind coast. It needed a lot of coasting. Down around six thousand feet we twisted the pipe off in the hole and they abandoned the well, paid us off, and said to come back in two months, maybe three months.

Benson, the little cockeyed driller, told me I'd made him a good hand. He said most big men were sloppy and slow on a drilling rig, but that I used my weight the way a small man does, and when he put down the next wildcat he thought I'd be ready to work derrick. He said I was too good to waste "down on the floor with the mules," and he wanted me upstairs with the wind in my hair and an extra two bits an hour on my paycheck. It was all I could do to keep from laughing in his face.

Now the hot soapy water in the old-timey bathtub in the little hotel in Krotz Springs felt lovely.

I hadn't had a hot-water bath in almost four months. The soap was oily and fragrant and it slid down my chest making little zeros of suds, each filled with the milky-green color of the water. I slumped down in the water so that my chin rested just on the surface of it. I soaped my head and scrubbed it with fingertips and fingernails, then ducked beneath the deep hot water, holding my breath, feeling the dirt of months float loose. I always cut my hair short, so short I can use it for a fingernail brush when I wash my head. I credit this trick to Washington and Lee University. It's about the only thing they taught me there in that splendid woman-starved nest of culture where students address one another as "gentleman," where freshmen wear nausea-atingly cute beanie caps, where no one walks on the neatly clipped grass, and everyone is so sporting it hurts.

The bellhop beat on the door of the bedroom while I was still underwater in the tub.

It surprised me that I could hear him. The noise came through the thick steel tub and through the water, a thumping, ringing sound. I surfaced and told him I would be there as soon as I dried myself, and he said all right in that weary, completely neutral voice peculiar to bellhops. While I was drying, he began knocking again, and I had the towel wrapped around me when I reached the bedroom door opening onto the flea-bitten corridor with its cheese-colored walls.

"Here she is," he said.

And there she was. I guess I'll always remember the first time I saw her, standing there in the half-gloom of the corridor, with the country-town bellhop dressed like an organ-grinder's monkey, almost leaning against her, smirking.

"She's a looker, ain't she, Bub?"

I said she was a looker. He appreciated that, smilingly, with a terrible show of teeth. He said he was glad I liked her and that she was the best there was in Krotz Springs and that God only knew why she bothered to hang around a little fishing village on the Atchafalaya when she could be in New Orleans or Memphis or anywhere, what with her legs and manners and all.

She said nothing.

Her eyes were lavender-gray and her hair was light creamy gold and springy-looking, hugging her head in curves rather than absolute curls. She wore a navy-blue beret of the kind you associate with European movies. Then there was the hair and face and a long loose stretch of metal-colored raincoat, very wet, and the cold smell of it plain in the mustiness. Then there were the legs and the bellhop wasn't kidding about them. Then there were the feet, broad and fat and short as a baby's. The shoes looked expensive, brown suede and shiningly wet.

"For God's sake give him his dollar," she said, putting no feeling into it one way or the other.

I moved to the bureau and got the dollar and gave it to the bellhop. He smiled awfully and left, and she came in and shut the door and there we were in the room together, just like that. We weren't—and then we were. After sixteen weeks on a drilling rig, it is a lovely shock to find yourself with no mud in your ears, alone in a room with a young expensive-looking woman with lavender-gray eyes.

"Hello," she said, still putting nothing into it.

I think I grinned. I remember that the Buster Keaton act didn't seem to fit the loveliness of the face, didn't seem to fit it at all, and when she plumped down on the iron starch of the top sheet of the bed, it crackled comically.

I said, "I'd've worn a nicer towel if I'd known this was going to be formal."

"I'm tired," she said. Her hands were cupped a-against the aluminum-colored rubber of the raincoat over her knees. "Let's don't make jokes."

"All right."

"Never joke with a tired tramp," she said. "No one gets as tired as a tired tramp."

She shivered and said she could do with a drink. I sloshed her a bourbon on rocks, using the bathroom glass and what was left of the ice. I made a lazy little ceremony of it, partly because the red-orange bourbon looked pretty as it thinned against the ice, and partly because I wanted the ice to dilute it a bit, and partly because my hands were clean for the first time in a long time and I liked the way the glass squeaked against my clean palms.

"It's good," she said, not making a face the way most women do with raw whisky.

"You mean it *was* good."

"I could do with another."

"From the looks of you, you could do with the whole fifth."

"Could do." She nodded. She looked me up and down. Not appraisingly or insultingly, but the way you look at a building or a mountain or an anthill, just looking. I stood there taking it, the thin grass carpet scratchy against the soles of my water-softened feet, looking back at her. I felt a laughable impulse to introduce myself and to dig into the classic parlor patter of home towns and possible mutual friends and to explain why I was wearing a towel and to tell her the bellhop had me all wrong, that what I wanted was a big stupid commercial blob of a woman; not a slender poised thing with skin the color of pearls melted in honey.

Instead I poured the drinks, this time mixed with tepid water.

The rain beat against the windows and against the tin roof of the hotel. It came down in hissing roars, then in whispers, then in loud shishes like sandpaper rubbed against wood. She drank the second glassful, climbed off the bed and began undressing, and then we were together, the cheap naked bulb still blazing down on the bed.

Thinking back, I remember the stupidest things; the way there was a taut crease just above her hips, in the small of her back. The way she smelled like a baby's breath, a sweet barely there smell that retreated and retreated, so that no matter how close you got to it you weren't sure it was there. The brown speckles in the lavender-gray eyes, floating very close to the surface when I kissed her, the eyes wide open and aware. But not caring. The eyes of a gourmet offered a stale chunk of bread, using it of necessity but not tasting it any more than necessary. I remember getting up and coming back to her, and of throwing a shoe at the light bulb, later, when the whisky was gone. I remember the smell of rain-darkness in the room and her telling me I'd cut my feet on the light-bulb glass on the floor. And how she said I was no better than a tramp myself, that I made love to the cadence of the rain gusts on the roof, and it was true I was doing just that, but it seemed the natural thing then. And I felt so marvelously clean and soaped and so in tune with the whole damned universe that I had the feeling I could have clouded up and rained and lightninged myself, and blown that cheese-colored room to smithereens.

~§~

I was up early next morning for more of the soap and water, and she came into the bathroom while I was still in the tub. She was dressed. She told me she was leaving and that it had been a nice night. This she said in the small, automatic voice of a child leaving a birthday party, her thoughts already somewhere else. Her eyes were clear, her lips a freshly painted red. The fact that I was bathing seemed to mean no more to her than the cracks in the tile wall.

I hauled out of the tub and picked her up and carried her back into the bedroom and it was three days before we left the room. Together. She said it was like the song we kept getting on the little bedside radio: "If You've Got the Money, Honey, I've Got the Time." The trashy tune and words sounded funny coming out of her in the Wellesley manner, in that imperceptibly clipped, ladylike voice.

"But when the money's gone," she said, "I'm gone, too. I don't sleep for thrills any more."

"Did you ever?"

She laughed. "Let's let it go at that; I just don't any more."

That was all right with me. After the months on the river I didn't feel finicky about the nuances of romance—all I wanted was plenty of it. At that time I had no more idea of falling in love with her than I had of making a meal of the big yellow cake of soap in the Victorian bathroom.

"When the money's gone," I told her, "I'll probably be sick of you."

"I hope so."

"Why?"

"It'll be better if you're sick of me." But like I say, when we left the hotel we left it together, the funny-faced old bellhop toting our bags out to my Packard convertible, carrying the bags a block to the parking lot down by the river, smirking every foot of the way.

I gave him a dollar and then another fifty cents when he'd got the bags squared away in the square-tailed trunk of the car.

The Packard was none the worse for storage, and at Alexandria I stopped at a used car lot and bought a pair of Louisiana tags with the white pelican on them. Just to play it safe. The man sold them fairly cheap and they had a nice comfortable shine to them after they were fitted into the nickeled frames.

Going across the Red River bridge, I sailed my Mississippi tags over the iron railing and saw them hit the water with a splash, forty feet below. She watched me, leaning back in her leather-padded corner, smoking quietly. Nothing seemed to surprise her: the car, the tags, the business of taking an uncharted trip with an unknown man. The wind whipped her bright hair the way it does in the soft-drink advertisements, cooperatively, beautifully. The cross-stripes of tar on the white highway thumped faster and faster beneath the wheels until the thumping became a buzzing. The air was soft; yet not dead. And over all of it lay the very good feeling of going somewhere.

Chapter Two

IN DALLAS I got turned around somehow and drove out through a plush Home-and-Garden-Club kind of neighborhood, where all the houses were of long thin wafers of Roman brick or blotchy fieldstone and were set far back from the road, their picture windows shining like gold foil in the late sun. We passed what must have been some kind of club, and there were limber-legged young kids on a strip of fine clay, stroking brand new white tennis balls with a beautiful laziness, their expensively coached strokes almost insolent. Then we came out of that part of town and there were some grubby youngsters batting an old gray ball around a gray asphalt court, a public one with ragged chicken-wire backstops. These kids played aggressively, jumpy and fast, the movements ugly and determined. They beat the ball as if they were killing a snake.

"It's funny," she said to me, "they can be playing the same game and yet an altogether different one. It's the money."

"Yes."

"Everything stinks without the money."

"Almost everything."

"Some day I'm going to wallow in it again. I'm going to strip down buck naked and bathe in cool green hundred-dollar bills."

"You said *again*."

"Did I?" She asked it teasingly.

"You tell *me*."

"What difference?"

"Oh, no difference," I said. "No difference at all. But you're a funny one, with your saddle-stitched shoes and your million-dollar luggage and half the time trying to talk like a ten-dollar tramp in that snooty voice. You're a comic."

"Don't be tiresome."

"That's what I mean, words like tiresome. I never in my life heard a tramp say tiresome."

She had lost interest. "Some day," she said, "I'm going to slosh around in hundred-dollar bills, new ones that've never been used before." She giggled, a small light sound against the heavy hum of the Packard. She was breathing oddly, her shoulders moving as if her lungs were upstairs there, in her shoulders. She wore a T-shirt of some kind of cocoa toweling and when she leaned back hard against the seat it was a splendid thing to see. Her skirt was gray flannel and it fitted as if it had been smeared on her, and below it were the legs. You hear and read about legs. But when you see the really good ones, you know the things you read and heard were a lot of trash.

I threw back my head and laughed and we swerved left, almost hitting a battleship-gray Olds '98, and the man and woman in it craned around to glare fleetingly at us. She stuck out her tongue at them. They blinked unbelievingly.

"Look at them," she said, "with their big prissy eight-thousand-a-year frowns."

She said she knew the man made eight thousand a year because he wore a button-down collar white oxford and when he frowned he did it just the way her eight-thousand-a-year uncle did it. As if he expected a bonus for it.

"That's not bad money," I said, feeling her out.

"There's no bad money."

"Oh?"

"But, darling, you've got to have drifts of it, lumps of it, and little piles of it only make you sick and petty."

It was the first time she'd called me darling and it was the first time she'd made anything approaching a speech on this my favorite subject. I eyed her with new interest. You can say what you want, but really money-hungry people, ravenously money-hungry ones, are a society all to themselves. My plan had been to get enough of her and to leave her in some filling station rest room between Dallas and Denver. I'd told her I was a salesman, that I sold novelties and notions to drugstores, and that the winter months were slack ones in the trade and I'd taken the roughnecking job on the river to tide me over. It's a funny thing, but I've found that if you tell someone you sell novelties and notions, they think it's impolite to ask what novelties and notions are. They don't ask you any more about it. Anyway, until she said there was no such thing as bad money, I was all for dumping her along the way in a day or so. Now I didn't know for sure, but I still thought I would, because a woman had no place in my plans. Most of them are big mouthed and easily identified. I don't know why, but you can pick any woman and she doesn't look as much like other women as a man looks like other men. Maybe it's the thousand different ways they can do their hair and lips. I don't know.

But this one with the cocoa-covered bosom and the absolutely perfect legs, a blind man could find her on a Friday noon in Rockefeller Plaza.

The road signs began making sense and we doubled back through the ritzy neighborhood and kept going north until we hit the highway I wanted.

That night we stopped at a barbecue stand where some kind of engine turned the beef ribs over and over, like a bloody Ferris wheel, over the charcoal fire. We ate slowly, washing down the greasy roasted meat with stingingly cold beer, and then we smoked and were quiet. I wanted some more potato salad and when we got it we decided to split it and get some more beer. The beer lasted longer than the salad. While we were finishing it, she moved over against me and I kissed her a long time, her lips cold and fresh and soft. She kissed the way an expert dancer follows the lead, giving and taking at exquisitely the right moment, and getting across the idea that she had a lot in reserve and this was only a sample. I'm not lying when I say I think that kiss lasted a quarter hour. But I still planned to leave her in the ladies John of some filling station. Because you can't kiss your way out of prison and I knew that for sure. For dead sure. And even as I kissed her I remembered way back in the dim part of my brain how it had been in solitary at Mississippi's Parchman. In solitary they shove your food to you through a hinged slit in the bottom of the door, and you don't get to see anybody, not anybody at all. I used to kick the tray back out through the slit and curse them, hoping they'd come in and beat me. Anything to break the monotony. But they didn't come. I'd shadowbox to kill time. There was no window, only the yellow light bulb with the juices of bugs on it, and I never knew if it was day or night or rain or shine or Sunday or what. You can't kiss your way out of a place like that, and there's no barbecue, no cold beer in there.

Still, though, if she could drive the way she loved . . . I gave her the wheel when we left the barbecue place and she curved out of the gravel drive as slick as anything you'd want to see. She handled the hydramatic shift without self-consciousness and she fed the heavy car the gas in a nice soft gush.

I smoked one more cigarette and went to sleep. I felt the good padded leather cool against my shoulders and I slipped down along the ribs of the leather, my knees into the dash, and I was back at Parchman, everything gray, the stone, the men, the air. The yard birds were moving around in the big oval enclosure after lunch, waiting for work call. The oval was inside three balconied levels and there was Shorty, up there on the third level the way he'd been last summer, holding onto the gray iron rail guard and yelling. He began beating his chest as I knew he would and he climbed up there on the railing and teetered a long second and then he did a perfect swan dive. Sixty feet below, he hit the paving on his chest and chin. It made a noise like nothing you've ever heard. Not loud. Not soft. I ran toward him, but there was a crowd and I couldn't get in because they were cleaning up and rolling him in a tarpaulin and the only thing I ever saw of him after he landed was the darker gray business on the light gray stone. It was so exactly the way it had been, with Jeepie out on the edge of the sweating crowd trying to bum a smoke and Thompson crying and saying that Shorty used to be an AAU high-board diver and it was the best way for him to die—with everyone looking. Thompson said Shorty did that swan into the stone just as nicely as if the judges were scoring him on points: "You see the way he held his feet together and his back hollow?" They had to take Thompson off somewhere, but the next day in the leather-goods shop he was his same old gray self and he never mentioned Shorty again in any way that I remember.

The dream unraveled into raspberry lipstick and lavender-gray eyes with speckles in them and a swirl of baby-smelling hair and the song on the radio: "If You've Got the Money, Honey, I've Got the Time." And then it looped back to the prison without any kind of transition or tapering. We wore the smutty blue uniforms of the guards and there was blood, sticky and fresh, on the left cuff of my stolen jacket, and we were walking toward the cement wall with the wooden ladder, Jeepie on the front end, me in the middle, and Thompson on the tail of the ladder. The light came down in a long clear tube from the lookout's post. It wavered behind us, curved beyond us, and then settled down on us. I could almost feel the cold heat of it and my eyes ached from the glare and my whole body ached from waiting to be shot. The lookout, said in an oddly conversational tone, "Who goes?" And Thompson waved up at the tower, and said, "It's all right. It's O.K." Then we were wedging the ladder against the concrete, the light from the tower still full on us, sparking against the quartz sand in the wall. Thompson and I were up and over the wall, and it was almost cold in the darkness on the other side, cold and quiet. I looked up and Jeepie was hanging up there with his belly against the stone. He was golden with the light and I could see his face and the forked vein high on his head. And there came a rattling from the tower, not a deadly sound or a dramatic one, a commonplace rattling like someone shaking rocks in a cigar box. And Jeepie's face became a tangle of shining black, a modernistic tangle of fluid and flesh where the bullets from the tower tore into it. It was still a face, but you couldn't tell where the eyes and mouth had been before the gun began rattling in the tower; then it wasn't a face at all and Thompson and I were running away from the wall.

I jumped, and when I opened my eyes she was pulling wide and to the left, smoothly, around a yellow diesel truck. We missed the truck by a good two inches and slid along and around it as if it were buttered, and she kicked the Packard up to eighty-five. I yawned and scratched my head, began looking for my cigarettes.

Having her at the wheel gave me a good feeling. She kept the left front fender pasted to the center stripe of the road, grooving it as if it were a rail. I fell asleep before I ever found the cigarettes. I dreamed again and this time Jeepie was talking all through it. His big plan. How many times I'd heard it. But he was talking now through the mouth the machine gun made for him and the words were squashed and wet. He said the first thing you had to do was buy yourself a trailer, a very harmless-looking one, wide in the beam, wide as the law would allow and maybe a little wider. It should be at least thirty-three feet long, he said, and the kind of trailer that didn't glitter or interest anyone. It had to be a boring kind of trailer, with a lived-in look, reeking of domesticity. It had to be a trailer with a few dents in it here and there and an old-fashioned hitch, no hydraulic gadgets for Jeepie and the big plan that died with him on top the wall. And, most important of all, the trailer must be like a box, with a straight, sturdy rear wall. The rear wall was the thing of things and Jeepie said wetly, with his poor bullet-made mouth, that if the wall was not right, none of it was right.

~§~

In Wichita Falls we made our first real stop, staying there three days in a dark lazy hotel with high-ceilinged rooms and clean, tiled baths. I got rid of the last hints of the mud moons under my finger-nails, and between us we got rid of three fifths of I. W. Harper and a lot of other things it wouldn't do to describe here. After the second day I felt as limber and light-legged as a goose and I was tired of eating in the room and so was she, so we went downtown and ate a couple of gray steaks in a place with a fine enameled front which advertised steaks as a specialty of the house.

After dinner we stopped at a jewelry shop and bought her a plain white-gold wedding ring. She wore no polish on the long round fingers and that somehow made them appear more nude, and the jewelry clerk seemed to have himself a hard time making up his mind to let go of them after he slipped on the ring. Maybe the ring was a laugh, and maybe it wasn't. Because, after all, we were going to be rooming together, at least until I left her, and hotel people are funny about slick fingers.

Then we went to a department store and I bought her a pink girdle that had wide panels in it and was several sizes too big for her. The panels were important, as important on a smaller scale as the sturdy rear wall of Jeepie's trailer. We bought her some jeans, too. And it was a good thing to see her trying on the jeans in front of the three-way mirror. She was all of a long slim golden piece, but there were sockets, too, like you see in *Vogue*, where the women by simply sticking out a leg in a certain way can make a denim rag look like something you ought to eat. The saleswomen in ladies' ready-to-wear cooed and giggled and smoothed, and she treated them with an easy friendliness.

With the jeans, she got a denim jacket that would have looked like a maternity smock on anyone else. On her it was alive and you could tell where she was and where she wasn't under all that coarse cloth. The expensive preoccupied smile dissolved and the eyes had a tilt to them and she practically dunked herself in the mirrors, the wedding ring shining like six million dollars.

That night, our last one in Wichita Falls, she ripped

the machine-stitched threads from the girdle and sewed seventeen hundred-dollar bills into the panels. In each of three panels there were four bills, and in the fourth there were five. The money represented everything I'd made on the drilling rig on the Atchafalaya River, plus a little I'd picked up here and there before I began roughnecking. It wasn't a lot, but I had a horror of being broke. I've always had this feeling about being without money. And there's this about a woman's girdle: it makes you think of various things, but none of these things is money. I told her we'd keep the girdle in the glove compartment of the Packard since, with her figure, she certainly didn't need it, and since, as I've said, I planned to ditch her at the right time and place.

I still had almost a hundred in my billfold and figured it would be more than enough to get us to Denver. We'd need the other money there. And if we used it right, or rather, if I used it right, I'd be living high on the hog for a long, long time.

Since the two of us left Krotz Springs I'd begin thinking occasionally in terms of "we." It irritated me; it smelled of softness, and I wanted none of it. Yet it kept popping up in my plans and making me madder and madder, so that by the time we reached Raton, New Mexico, I decided it was time to jettison my friend with the cream-colored hair.

It proved so simple as to be almost disappointing.

On the outskirts of Raton, at the foot of the mountain pass, we pulled into this cafe-filling-station place and went inside for coffee.

We'd seen the empty Greyhound bus out front and the cafe was jammed with bus passengers. They were eating sandwiches and drinking coffee in the quick listless way people do when they've been told they have only fifteen minutes to spruce up and get themselves fed. There were a few tables with black plastic tops which shone in swirls where they'd been wet-rubbed. There was a counter with white stools and the counter ran at right angles to a whisky and beer bar at the south end of the room.

When we came in, the noise quieted, the men looking at her, the single ones staring and the married ones looking out the sides of their eyes as if it didn't matter too much to them about her being there. But looking just the same. There was no arguing that she had it, and that whatever it was, she beamed it out solid and steady as a revolving beacon. And if you didn't actually see it, you still felt the warmth of it and wondered.

I took her arm, hating myself for the silly sheltering gesture, and said, "Let's get a drink first." There was less of a crowd at the bar than at the food counter.

She wrinkled her nose. "I think we've been drinking too much. To enjoy drinking, you've got to *not* drink for a while. Contrast."

"You be contrasty, I'm having a drink."

There was a medium-young fellow on one of the white stools at the food counter, and as we talked, he swung around to watch her. He had thick bluish-black Hollywood sideburns and he wore a suit that was too tweedy and New England for the month of May in New Mexico. It had so many flap pockets on the jacket that he looked like a ventilator.

She made a pretty show of looking through her purse for something, pouting the way a woman with a good mouth can pout. Then she said she was going out to the car to get cigarettes from where she'd left them on the seat and she'd be right back and for me to go ahead with the drink and she would join me. She gave me a radiant smile and the door slammed behind her and then I was ordering my I. W. Harper at the varnished bar. As smiles go, the one she'd given me was a fine one, but it was cold, too, if you know what I mean, plenty of stretch in the lips but no eyes or heart in it. Like her lovemaking. Mechanically splendid, yet as though the performance was the result of some remote control and did not really involve her. The double shot hit bottom with a gentle explosion at about the same time she returned to the cafe.

She strolled to a vacant stool at the food counter and the Hollywood sideburns began taking bites out of her with his eyes. He sat to her left. There was a fat woman in a little-girl dress of checkered cotton between them, but he leaned forward and twisted and stared.

The bus passengers began filing out, some of them taking pieces of sandwiches and cookies with them.

I had another drink and when I looked around again the fat woman was gone and this tweedy joker with the pockets napping all over him was talking to my passenger. She wasn't saying anything. But then again she wasn't shrinking, and it hit me that now was as good a time as any to chop the thing off clean, to leave her there on the porcelain stool and get the hell on to Denver. The bartender was looking at me strangely, half amused and half worried. A fly strutted around the rim of my empty glass, a purplish fly with a back that changed color like the plumes in a rooster's tail. Those things come back especially sharp, clearer than the way she looked or the way I felt.

I moved away from the bar and to the door, very slowly, and she didn't turn around.

The Packard kicked off nicely, and when I got the wheels out of the gravel and onto the road I pushed her hard for maybe a minute, whistling, "If You've Got the Money, Honey, I've Got the Time." Before it had sounded whimsical and frank and functional. Before it had sounded gay and uncomplicated. Now the tune had a nasty taste to it.

"Well," I said to the dashboard, "*I've* got the money and *I've* got the time."

I laughed and the hot New Mexico wind blew it out of my mouth and out the window before it started. I threw back my head and laughed louder, but it didn't come off any better. I pulled over to the side of the road to get at my extra cigarettes in the glove compartment.

The five packs were in there, along with a miniature flashlight I use in my work, and the .357 Magnum Smith and Wesson revolver. But the thing that wasn't in there where it belonged was the pink girdle we'd bought in Wichita Falls.

Stuff was stacked all around the place where the girdle had been folded. I never saw a bigger, blacker hole than the one in there where the girdle had been.

I sat without moving, my fist in the glove compartment, my mouth hanging open. The back of my fist was sweating. I forced myself to think back deliberately, very deliberately, to her leaving the cafe, and then to how she came back, her tiny bag swinging from the slim strap over her wrist. You couldn't stuff a girdle in a handbag no bigger than a hamburger. And she'd been just as cool as a cantaloupe, sitting there at the counter, her cheek half turned to that guy; picture of a lady more interested in a ham sandwich than in anything else in the world. She had more than six thousand ham sandwiches in that girdle. And she had the girdle on. The cold-blooded little blonde was crackling with my hundred-dollar bills.

I don't remember jerking the car around in the road and heading back to Raton. I don't remember the ride at all.

The bus was no longer in front of the cafe and there were no cars there. There was an old fellow, wearing puffy pants like the Canadian Royal Mounties, standing beside the lone gas pump, beating on it with his hand as if something had gone wrong with the dial that registered the gallons. He paid no attention to me, and when I came out of the place he was still slapping at the pump.

"Uncle, have you seen a blonde in jeans and a man about my height in a brown suit?"

Whap! He slapped the glass face of the gauge, ignoring me.

"A brown hairy suit?" I went on. "I asked inside and they told me this blonde left with the man in the brown suit, and I've got to find them quick because her mother is sick and wants her to come right away." My tongue felt thick and dry.

Tunk, tunk, tunk. He hit the metal part of the pump with the heel of his hand.

I reached out and grabbed him by the front of his shirt and lifted him up against me, and said, "Listen, damn you, if you don't tell me whether you saw my girl go off with that punk in the brown suit—"

"Why didn't you say so, son?" he said in a reasonable voice. "I didn't know she was your girl."

"Which way'd they go? And in what?"

"Wal, her and this *hombre* jumped into one a them low-down Englishy things without no top—he had it parked over yonder in the shade—and they sat there arguin' a bit and seemed like fer a while she was goin' to climb back right smack outa that car."

"Spare me the Western color, Uncle. What color was the car? And which way?"

"Thataway." He seemed disappointed. "I think it was purple, blackish purple."

I retraced the road we'd taken from Cartersville to Raton, moving along at a brisk clip but not too fast to check the sweep of flat fawn-colored land to either side of the highway. The .357 Magnum was in my lap and I picked it up and thumbed the cylinder release so that the cylinder swung out to the left, heavy with its load of brass and lead.

I dumped the cartridges out in the V of my legs against the leather of the seat and, still driving, I flipped the cylinder back into anchorage and dry-fired the gun at the windshield. The double action was nice and oily, with just enough tension and delay. The .357 Magnum is a work of art, just about the size and bore of a .38 caliber, but with approximately double the power of penetration. It is a fancy-shooting, but not a fancy-looking gun, and if you lay it on something and squeeze it off slowly, that something is going to fall.

I refilled the chambers with one hand and pushed the gun in the waistband of my pants and buttoned my coat over it. By this time I'd hit the edge of Cartersville, a town of typical flat-topped Indian-style houses and little curio shops with signs saying:

"come in and see giant
MAN-KILLING LIZARD," and
"SEE THE MAN-DESTROYING RATTLESNAKE," and
"REAL LIVE COBRA—COBRAS KILL A MAN EVERY
HOUR IN INDIA."

Virginia had told me—did I tell you her name was Virginia?—that one summer she visited her brother in Albuquerque and he explained how the signs worked. Most of the lizards and snakes were stuffed. But the signs were interesting, and after you stopped and went inside the curio shop and saw all the beaten coin-silver splashed with turquoise and obsidian you were likely to buy yourself twenty or thirty dollars worth of Zuni bracelets. She said the snakes and lizards were no more dishonest than the stinking dead whales in carnival side shows and, anyway, the lizards led you to the Zuni jewelry and it was very good. Imaginative and delicate, not a bit like the sluggish squares and ovals and swastikas the Pueblo tribe turns out. Well, she had enough folding money in the girdle to buy herself a turquoise igloo, or hogan, or whatever it is they live in out there. The gun felt solid and warm against my leg.

Just inside the town, to the right of the road, I saw this sprawling adobe building rimmed with neon tubing, and a sign out front advertising steaks and drinks and dancing. The neon tubing was very dead and curly in the sunlight, like old fingernail parings pasted against the mud.

There were three cars in the drive, two Buicks and a plum-colored XK-120 Jaguar sports job.

Inside, it was hot, but the gloom gave an illusion of semi-coolness and it was a moment or so before the holes in my eyes opened up enough to let me see anything much. They were in a booth, sipping some kind of crushed-ice things through straws, the Hollywood sideburns talking fast and low between sips. She was listening, but not making an exercise of it.

Beyond them, in a corner of the room, was a juke-box framed and ornamented with neon, squirting salmon-and-white light into the artificial twilight of the room. Some high-powered thrush was skipping through "Kiss of Fire," singing it fast and impatiently, as if she had to catch a train. I moved across what must have been the dance floor and then I was sitting there in the booth beside her, looking across the table at her friend. He stopped talking and concentrated on me and the drink. I reached across the table and took the drink from him, threw the straw on the floor, and drank whatever it was in the glass.

He put his elbows on the table and thought about it. Virginia kept sipping.

I didn't like the drink and said so. He balled his fist, a large one and nicely tanned, but then he scratched his head with his knuckles, lightly, careful not to dislodge any of the thick hairdo. Then he thought about it some more.

"Tim," Virginia said sweetly, "this is Nick something-or-other."

No one said anything.

"And Nick," Virginia finally said to her friend, "this is Tim. You may call him Timothy."

I chewed a cheekful of the perfumed ice from the glass before saying: "This is really shaping up as a party."

"Fine," Nick said, turning to Virginia. "And he may call me Nicholas."

"I know we're going to have a good time," I said, "I can feel it coming on." The ice made a lot of noise. The thrush in the jukebox became wilder and wilder and there was a thumping as if she were hurling herself against the plastic walls of the box. She went off the air in a series of clicks and metallic hiccups and was replaced by a sleepy Negroid voice, this one male, yawning its way through "Tenderly." Or maybe it was "Rhapsody." After all, it's been a long time and a lot of hell and happiness in between.

"I don't think this is going to do," Nick said finally. "I don't think it's going to do at all." He was swelling up to fill his coat, coming up off the bench of the booth by degrees. You could tell from the look on his face that he considered this psychological warfare at its best. Virginia just sipped away, not raising her eyes. Nick began sliding around the corner of the table, now very businesslike and quick, until he happened to look down at the edge of the table near my belly and he saw the working end of the .357 Magnum resting there. He laughed and plopped down on the bench. "That's different," he said,

I bumped the snout of the gun daintily on the table. "Oh my, yes, it's altogether different."

"Isn't it?" Virginia said, filling the two words with amusement and contempt.

"Nicholas," I said, "I want you to wipe your chin

and go out there and get in your Jaguar and start rolling."

Virginia did something with her glass, rattling the ice. "Once at Krotz Springs I told Tim he looked a great deal like a great big John Garfield, and I don't think he ever will get over it. Now he even gets into his undershirts like John Garfield. He even sweats like John Garfield, with a nice photogenic shine." She giggled.

"Garfield's dead," Nick said.

I bumped the gun on the table, a little harder this time. "Nicholas, I want to apologize for the short honeymoon, and I'll be seeing you. They tell me a Jaguar will do eighty-five in second gear."

Virginia giggled again, saying, "Oh, yes, we'll be seeing you. You must visit us in Krotz Springs during the oil-well season."

Then we were outside, Nick walking ahead of us and getting into the plum-painted Jaguar without looking at Virginia. He did not do eighty-five in second, but then again he did not mess around, and I imagine the cheap white-gold wedding ring must have been almost as big in his mind as the gun. The insides of my arms felt clammy and my ribs prickled with relief. What I'd wanted least at this point was trouble, trouble of any kind, with anybody. All my plans hinged on remaining as unnoticed as possible, anyway as unnoticed as you could be with a woman like Virginia along. As she climbed into the Packard I slapped her on the rump, making it look playful and marital in case anyone was watching from the front door of the adobe building.

I breathed easier then. She was wearing it—the girdle.

We turned around and headed again for Raton Pass, not stopping this time at Raton, but going on until the road widened and smoothed out for the long climb over the mountains and into Colorado. The trees got shorter and skinnier and the grass thinner. The air crisped and cooled despite the sunshine, which near the peak of the pass seemed almost to crackle among the rocks.

These things registered with me because I am something of a fool about the outdoors. I feel the same way about the sky and clouds, and being able to move around, as an evangelist feels about religion. I guess freedom and the money to enjoy it are a kind of religion, a very exclusive kind. No matter. I kept thinking about the girdle and looking around for a place isolated enough to stop the car and grab her and peel that seventeen hundred dollars worth of silk and rubber and paper off those obscenely perfect hips. And at the same time I kept comparing the rocks and the sky with what we have down South and kind of gloating to think that the South, though lacking in chamber-of-commerce promotion, has the subtlest colors and teasing-est smells a man could want. Out West all the smells are sucked up out of the baked land by the sun. And it's as if all the colors in the ground are gobbled up by their sunsets, and so is the blue of the sky. The sky is high and pale and impersonal and you get the feeling it doesn't belong to you at all, but that it is the property of the chamber of commerce. In the South the sky is humid and low and rich and it's yours to smell and feel. In the West you're only an observer. In the West someone sees a flower growing on a mountain and he writes a whole damned pamphlet about it. In the South the roses explode out of the weeds in the yards of the poorest shanties. Blood red ones. And pink ones—pink as that new girdle. Nature or no nature, the girdle was the thing. But the cars kept passing in both directions. That Raton Pass is a busy place.

We crossed the pass and stopped for gas in Trinidad, Colorado, and Virginia said she wanted to go to the ladies room, but I said no, we'd go on down the road a piece and find us a cabin. She laughed and didn't argue.

On the other side of Trinidad, at about dusk, I saw the kind of place I'd been looking for, a rough little road that bent off to the left. I swung onto it and bumped along a quarter mile or more making sure it didn't lead to a roadside park or anything else that would attract people. I braked to a halt, left the lights blazing against a blank red wall of rock. The light bounced back in the car under the canvas top and I could see she was grinning. She said, "The girdle?"

"Yes, ma'am."

She lit a cigarette. "No, Tim, I don't think so." The

smoke curled around the words. "You're so damned complacent I think I'll make you work for it."

"That's all right."

I pushed my arm between her back and the seat and began pulling her to me and she hit me in the mouth with her right fist, hard. I tasted blood, and then she was out of the car and running. She ran maybe twenty yards and kicked off her shoes and then she really ran. Up the slope and beyond the spray of the headlights, moving neat and swift as a boy. The girdle didn't seem to slow her. She cleared a fairly big rock just beyond the edge of the light and I piled out and started after her.

We were running through knee-high stuff which had a rubbery feel to it when I caught up with her and tackled her and we both balled up in the stuff when we fell, Virginia laughing as if it were the funniest thing in the world to be out there on the mountain in the moonlight fighting over a new girdle. She tried to hit me again, but this time I blocked it with my wrist and slapped her high on the cheek. She kept struggling and I hit her again, lower, on the side of the neck.

Then she began fighting in earnest. It scared me.

I didn't want to cut loose and belt her, but I had to have the money. I knew if I hit her in the throat or on the bridge of the nose or even on the temple, I might cave the bone and kill her. I didn't want to leave any dead woman up there in the rocks. All I wanted was quiet, and to go on to Denver and get me the kind of trailer Jeepie said you ought to get if you wanted to be rich. But she kept rattling those hard little fists off the side of my head and beating me in the face. I weighed in the neighborhood of a hundred and ninety-eight, and I don't guess she'd've weighed in at more than a hundred and eighteen if the girdle had been loaded with silver dollars. But trying to strip the thing off her was like trying to skin a baby python with a sledge hammer for a head.

It was a long time before I even got her out of the jeans.

I'd wedged my fingertips under the rubber then, the backs of my knuckles digging roughly into her, but the girdle refused to start rolling. Then suddenly she bridged her back and I jerked very fast, so that the stretchy material came down and over my thumbs. After that it was easier, but I was still taking a hell of a beating and once she drove her knee against my nose and the darkness buzzed with off-color lights. It was too much. When I had the girdle clear of her bare feet I reared up on my knees and hit her, putting all the pain of my nose into it. She kept moving around and I slammed my fist into her face again and I didn't care if the whole FBI was hiding in the rocks with a portable electric chair.

She pulled me down against her in the strange tall mountain bushes where I'd tackled her and for the first time she loved me the way I'd hoped she would—no remote control, no cool technical performance. She held, me in the tight jerky way a girl holds a man, her first man—or a new man.

And when I rolled over on my back that great big chamber-of-commerce moon was curdled with purest gold.

Chapter Three

WE SPENT THE NIGHT in Pueblo and it was a night I like to think about, especially now that my time is so short and sometimes I get to thinking that twenty-seven years is not very many years to have lived. When I get to thinking like that, the memory of the night in Pueblo is a kind of tonic I can't explain. After all, no matter how long you live, there aren't too many really delicious moments along the way, since most of life is spent eating and sleeping and waiting for something to happen that never does. You can figure it up for yourself, using your own life as the Scoreboard. Most of living is waiting to live. And you spend a great deal of time worrying about things that don't matter and about people that don't matter and all this is clear to you when you know the very day you're going to die. Take me, for instance. I've always been scared to death of cancer and once I was sure I had cancer of the lung.

And for a year I've fretted having a tooth filled because when anything cold hits it the thing bothers me. But I'll never die of cancer of the lung and I won't have to go to the dentist with that tooth. Now I know that. Now I know how much of the twenty-seven years was pure junk. So when I'm reeling off the things I've done and haven't done, way back in my head, I take that night in Pueblo and look at it over and over; the way you'll go to a movie you like, catching it at two or three different houses to see if it is as good as you thought the first time.

I think of the way we split our drinks, pouring only one at a time and snaring it till it was gone, and swapping the ice back and forth from her mouth to mine. I think of the way we laughed at ourselves and how the girdle, still packed with the money, hung from the overhead light fixture. The fixture was one of those hideous three-pronged ones, covered with steel leaves which were painted in various tones of mildew. The girdle was speared on one of the sharp leaves and cast a shadow across her.

In the daylight we reviewed the damage, too tired and sick to think it funny; but not too sick to eat the sausage and eggs and toast at the little restaurant that was part of the tourist court. Her right eye was puffed and her lips were bruised and cut. My nose was swollen and bloodshot where she'd banged me with her knee on the mountain. Furthermore, during the four or five hours we'd slept she had chilled out again, and she looked across the coffee cup at me as if we'd just been introduced and she hadn't quite made up her mind about me. Most of the time we were at breakfast she was reading the morning paper, the *Pueblo Chieftain*, sticking to the front page of it. There was a big black splash about the New York district attorney rooting into a call girl syndicate where the girls received as much as five hundred dollars a night for their favors. And there was a large picture of a babe with a knockout figure and a polka-dotted shawl or something over her face. I'd bought the paper and glanced at it before giving it to Virginia. At the time I thought her interest in the story was mostly because of the money angle.

There was no talk.

I paid the check and tipped the waitress, who was hanging over the table like a fat starched cloud. I smiled at Virginia and she folded up the newspaper. The car ran nicely and the girdle was locked in the glove compartment with the gun and cigarettes. It was a fine day, we were free and on the move, and aside from this, I'd made a fairly important decision about her. I'd decided she was cocky and cool enough to help me with the trailer and the rest; and what with her ability to drive an automobile, and her guts, between the two of us we had a better than fair chance of swinging Jeepie's wonderful plan. He'd always said the plan called for two people, one on the waiting end, one on the dying end. Well, I had two people. Me and Virginia. And, God knows, the job, if handled without faltering at any stage of it, would net a big enough haul for a whole platoon of people. Jeepie always thought in hundreds of thousands of dollars. He looked like a shine boy and he thought in hundreds of thousands. Virginia would be on the waiting end. I didn't mind the dying end. Because back there I never thought about how a man could die by the clock and calendar, ticking off the days and the minutes as if he were waiting to have a baby. When I thought of dying there was a lot of noise in it and then blackness, no different than any other blackness but more complete and lasting. The way I had it doped, dying was pretty stagy and certainly not lonely.

So, the worst that could happen for me would be a good long sleep, this on the heels of a blaring final scene, replete with smell of cordite and criminal courage. And the worst for Virginia would be life in some state pen, guilty of conspiracy and subject therefore to the death penalty, but with the kind of legs and eyes juries do not like to burn. She would pull no trigger, swing no knife. She would wait—and drive. And life sentences have a way of becoming ten- or twenty-year sentences in the land of the free and the home of the brave. Five good soggy editorials would do it. Five painstaking interviews with the lady with the lavender-gray eyes, who knew her boy friend wasn't exactly legal, but who never thought he'd kill anybody for a dirty old mess of money. Parole for Virginia. More men for Virginia. Probably rich men, the kind who must have bought her the handbag with the lump of tortoise shell on it and the good shoes. And she'd treat them, too, like a gourmet chewing a hunk of stale bread. Or would she?

What in the devil had hounded her into taking a ten-dollar-a-call job in a backwoods hotel? She was running, too, but from what?

I found a parking space half a block from a sporting goods store, killed the engine, and removed the key from the ignition. It was midmorning and the sidewalk was nice and empty and I enjoyed the way it felt under my feet.

I told the man in the store what I wanted and he said he had just the thing I had in mind, a real goose-down sleeping bag with room for two, and that if the price was too stiff, he had some reclaimed single slee-per Army bags with brown blanket linings. I told him the new civilian goose-down bag was fine. I liked the way it was quilted so the feathers would shift around beneath the cloth.

He bundled the bag in brown paper and twine, rolling it small and tight in the package, and before I left he managed to sell me a Rogers pocketknife with a buck-horn handle and Sheffield steel blades. I didn't need the knife, but I've always liked to buy good things whether I need them or not, and the knife was like that.

The sleeping bag was something else. I figured since both of us were wearing lumpy faces it would be best not to stop at any hotels or cabins. You generally notice the face of a person who's been in a fight, no matter how uninteresting the face. Scatter a few lumps on it and you remember all the rest of it. Of course we'd have to stop now and then for food, but I could buy it in batches at country stores and make it last a long time.

The fewer persons who saw our bruised faces, the better for Virginia and me. We'd likely be coming back over this same road in a month or so.

I bought a fly rod and a few lures and some tackle and I bought a black Plumb hatchet in a soft leather case, and by the time I got back to the car she was dozing, the newspaper spread on her lap. I stowed the stuff in back as quietly as I could and rolled on down the street a couple of blocks and stopped again. There was a Kress store and next to it a cash-and-carry grocery. I picked up what we needed and when I came back she was smoking and looking at the Pan-Am map of Colorado, tapping it with one of those long nude-looking fingernails and now and then staring out the window as if she were a million miles away. She didn't watch me as I put away the frying pans and the lard and the rest of the stuff.

"Baby," I said, "we're going to do us some camping until our faces grow together."

She scratched the map absently. "And why do we want our faces grown together?"

"I mean in one piece. Mine in one piece and yours in one piece."

"Well," she said, "I'm in no hurry. I'm no camper, but I'm in no hurry."

"Good."

"But if you're dead set on crawling off in the rocks and munching wild locusts and licking your wounds, this looks like a good place for it." She was tapping the map again, and I slowed the car and saw that she was tapping a tiny-printed place, fuzzy with the markings the map people make to represent mountains. I liked the way it sounded—Cripple Creek. It sounded right for us.

"I had a friend," she went on, "who spent a whole summer there and came back raving about it. She said they had only one hotel. The Imperial, I believe. And that early every morning the people in the hotel took little miners picks out in the rocks and hacked away looking for gold until they were hungry. And then they ate what she called a prospector's breakfast. Fried burro meat and scrambled eggs."

"No one fries burro meat," I broke in, laughing.

"Maybe it was bacon. Anyway they beat on the rocks until they were starved and then they cooked and ate outdoors and went around climbing over old heaps of slag and mine tailings and peering down abandoned mine shafts."

"We don't want to stop at a hotel, that's what I was trying to tell you a while ago."

"And at night they sat around the lobby staring at their rocks."

"Fine."

"Or they went down in the basement of the hotel and watched an old-timey melodrama and got drunk and threw popcorn at the villain, who was a student at Cornel in the winters."

"No hotel for us." I wasn't thinking of what I was saying now. I was thinking of what she said about *peering down abandoned mine shafts*. It answered a question that had been nibbling away at the edges of my mind ever since I decided to buy the trailer. If such a shaft happened to be in a lonely enough spot, and if it was big enough and deep enough and dark enough— But this much was certain: I would want to do a little peering myself before I fitted it into the plan. One crooked piece in the puzzle and it would blow up in my face. Yet if I played it cold and smart, the good fat life was waiting for me. Five hundred, or five million dollars, the penalty for stealing it is the same, and it's better to do your thinking beforehand than afterward. If you can . . .

We left the main road at Colorado Springs and took to the mountains, the evening breeze cool and dry with a fresh spank to it. The road changed from concrete to crushed rock and later to gravel, with long irregular splotches of macadam. There was the damnedest sunset, smeared like syrup of opals over everything and dripping off the clouds the way the molten metal comes out of the ladle in a steel mill.

It lit up Virginia's face and filled the car with pink.

She was reading the front page of the Pueblo news-paper again and I wondered how she could keep her mind on it in that fine sea of pinkness and with so much to look at outside the car.

And from time to time I kept thinking of the aban-doned mine shafts. There must be some kind of trail leading to them. Some way to get in and out of the old locations. When you tore gold out of the ground you had to go somewhere with it. I'd read that some of the historic shafts in Colorado were so deep you could drop a pebble in them and light a cigarette before the pebble hit the water down there in the darkness. Or maybe that was in Montana. Sometimes people fell in them and were pulled on down and down into the under-ground workings, lost in a maze of water-filled tunnels, bobbling through eternity. No fish to eat them, though. Probably preserved in the ice water in that insane and forgotten blackness.

I looked around at Virginia to ask her to light me a cigarette. She was watching me, the folded paper in her lap. There seemed to be a certain agitation in her, but something deeper than her standard petulance, very little of it on the surface.

I smiled. "What's the matter?"

"I don't know," she said, shivering. "But I think you know. Isn't that funny?"

"Yes."

"I was just sitting here reading and then I started thinking again about Cripple Creek and that little hotel.

I was wondering how it felt to throw popcorn at the villain. And then the goose flesh popped out and the look on your face was all tied up with it."

I reached over and patted the back of her hand. She pulled away—her hand was cold. Mental telepathy? You tell me. All I know is Virginia's hand was cold and she didn't want me touching it. When she lit the cigarette for me, she passed it in such a way that our fingers didn't meet, and she kept watching me as long as there was any of the sunset left inside the car.

The road into Cripple Creek from Colorado Springs is a winding one with tightly bent horseshoes on three or four different levels before you reach the town in its green cup of valley. There is something crazy and happy and careless about the air and I don't think anybody can be gloomy up there for long, no matter how strange and big are their plans. In the twilight we got none of its color that first night, but it is very beautiful and the kind of country that is all tip-tilted, half of it standing on edge so you can really see its creases and ravines and spaces. If there is any place in the West that is almost as fine as the South, it is Cripple Creek and the country around it.

The sun dropped beyond the rock rim while we were still an eighth of a mile above the town. We could see the yellow lights down there, most of them hugging the ground, but a few sticking up higher and Virginia said that must be the Imperial Hotel.

There was a kind of half-circle gouged in the side

of the mountain at one point, where the road was maybe five times as wide. To the left of this curved space, a thinner road climbed into the dark.

We spent that first night up there.

Part II

Chapter Four

I FOUND SOME DEAD PINON WOOD and built a small fire in a hollow rock and then I got the hatchet and frying pans and coffee pot and bacon and eggs out of the back of the car and placed all these things in a neat row around the edge of the rock. Pinon wood has a lovely smell when it burns. With the hatchet I chopped an armload of it and brought it back and stacked it at the base of the rock. The rock was about three feet across at the top where the hollow part held the fire. It was almost waist-high. When the wind blew over the hollow the flames lay down against the coals and then they stood up and flapped and you could hear them, like cloth fluttering in the wind.

Virginia seemed very tired, and before I laid the skillet on the coals I pulled the new sleeping bag out of the car and fixed it for her a half-dozen paces from the fire where a baby cliff of stone leaned out over the little clearing. She crawled into the bag without undressing. Twice that night I touched her and each time she moved away from me so I decided the hell with it.

Toward midnight I was hungry again and I piled out of the bag and found some bologna and bread. Up there in those mountains your belly feels brand new, like you never used it before and can never get it full, and that stuff tasted like smoked turkey and biscuits. I washed it down with tepid coffee and walked around a while. A hundred yards up a crooked foot trail I found a fast shallow creek. Because of the wind you couldn't hear it until you were right on it. The water was all purple and brass and silver in the moonlight. I lay down and drank from the creek.

I went back to camp and poured the coffee I'd bought at the store into one of the inner sheets of the newspaper Virginia brought from Pueblo. I wrapped the loose coffee, folding it firmly in the sheet of paper so the grains of coffee would not spill. I took the shiny empty can up the grade to the creek and rinsed it, smelling it until it smelled only of water, then filling it with the freezing water and taking it to Virginia. She wasn't asleep. She drank half the can, pushed it away, and lay down and rolled over, without speaking.

After that I picked up the rest of the newspaper and took it in the car and read the front page again, using for light the tiny torch that hung from the ring with my car keys. The streamer story said that the New York D.A. believed there were two or three other call girls who had been forewarned of the crackdown on the syndicate, and who had left New York a few days before the raids began.

And farther down there was a piece that read something like this:

One of the girls still sought by the law, the district attorney said, is a prominent figure in local cafe society, and reputedly the former mistress of a big-time underworld figure.

The district attorney declined to give her name but described her as a blonde with violet eyes, an elegant manner, and a figure to match.

He said she was last seen by the doorman at her plush apartment house on Beekman Place, climbing into a taxi and "apparently in quite a hurry." The doorman said she took two bags with her and gave Grand Central station to the driver as her point of destination . . .

I folded the paper carefully into a compact square and locked it in the glove compartment with the girdle and the cigarettes and the gun. The wind had quieted when I fell asleep.

I woke up about a quarter to five and the light was already good, pale and steady without a hint of breeze. I eased out of the bag and stood there a minute looking down at her, then put on my pants and shoes and went to the car for the cheap fly rod and tackle and the other things, careful not to slam the door of the car. I tucked the gun in my waistband. I cut the money from the panels in the girdle and folded the bills into the hip pocket of my pants. Just in case. Then I relocked the glove compartment.

Wading the stream was not unpleasant. It was clear and for a while it didn't reach above my knees. It was cold, but a good clean cold, and the sun had begun warming the tips of the mountains. After more than a quarter-hour I came to a pool scalloped out of the living rock. I rigged the rod and flexed it. After a couple of experimental casts halfway across the pool I laid one near the far edge of it, close to an overhang of dark granite, exactly where I wanted it. Dropping the fly just where you want it is half the fun.

And I can say it without bragging, that when you put a Southern fly fisherman out there in those wide-open Western streams with no bushes or branches overhead and nothing to do but hit the target, he will hit it. A good Southern fly fisherman is the best there is, because he's used to watching out for cotton-mouths with one eye and trees and bushes and yellow jackets and God knows what all with the other, and making the cast by feel and prayer. But though I put the fly where I wanted it, nothing happened. I whipped it out there again and this time a rainbow took it in a smooth silver rush, spit it out, and left me.

He must have told his friends about me. Another

half-hour netted me nothing but two shoesful of water.

Finally I'd had enough of it and climbed out. I moved around the pool on the bank to the granite overhang and there were rough notches up the rim of it like stairs and you could see the sun was steaming hot up top, some forty feet above the surface of the pool, a fine place to dry my shoes and socks.

If I took my time maybe Virginia would cook breakfast, although she looked less like a cooker of breakfasts than anyone I ever knew. I reviewed the night before and the way she hadn't even thanked me for the water. My stomach growled. I decided if she were cooking her own meal when I returned I'd take it away from her and eat it. She was a lousy little tramp. God knows I'm an authority on tramps.

I whipped most of the sand and water out of my socks against the rock, then pasted them against it and drained my shoes, the brown dye coming out of the shoes with the water. There was a long spread of valley north of Cripple Creek and although I couldn't see the town from where I sat I could feel it, and I could see the final kink in the road where it bent into town. To the west of me, maybe two-hundred yards, there was a pile of slag glinting in the sun, only I didn't know it was slag at that time. And there was a weather-bleached outbuilding of some kind, tall and skinny and leaning, and some rusted machinery, a wheel of some kind in a tangle of cable near the building.

The wet shoes were warm and not too squishy as I

came down off my perch.

The closer I got to the old building the less sense it made to me, until I saw the yawning mouth of the shaft, its edges crumbling in the sun. Then I knew what it was. Ten yards from the hole I laid down the rod and slipped the gun out of my pants, laying it beside the rod, and edged forward on all fours.

There seemed to be an updraft, a current of air rising from the shaft, and I could feel it against my face and chest before I got a good look into the thing. When I managed finally to get my head over the edge, the chill was more distinct.

I dropped a rock, waited, heard nothing.

Two more rocks and nothing, then a bigger rock and a long wait and at last a faint plink. Like when you open your mouth and thump the side of your cheek with your finger. I crawled away from that place.

She was lying on the sleeping bag in the sun, as slim and bare as a sword, the light bouncing off her in sweet hard curves, the cream-colored hair in a pony tail, eyes closed. She'd turned the bag over so that she lay on the diamond-quilted back of it and the clear color of her against the tan cloth was beautiful to see.

There were hot coals in the hollow rock and the coffee was bubbling there in the cheap pot. There was some bacon, red and wrinkled, on a folded paper on the rim of the rock, and the bread was there in its oiled wrapper. I finished off the coffee, ate all the cooked bacon and the bread, sitting with my back against the cooking rock and looking at her. I didn't know whether or not to tell her about the shaft. I felt remarkably happy because the shaft was such a big one as well as such a deep one and then, too, I felt happy because of the walloping stretch of space all around me, the feeling of freedom up there in the rocks. You don't know the meaning of freedom until you've been locked up a long time.

I dumped the grounds out of the coffeepot, burned the bread wrapper and the paper she'd used as a blotter for the bacon grease. I smoked and the taste of it was a sweetness like nothing in this world. I gave her a cigarette and she propped up on her elbows to smoke it, kicking her toes lightly against the bag. "Tim, you'll find out anyway, so I might as well tell you."

"Tell me what?"

"I took the hatchet and beat hell out of the glove compartment in the car. I tried to pry it open but it wouldn't come. And I beat hell out of it."

"And what did that get you?"

"It got me a girdle, the one you slit to pieces."

I kept smoking.

"Tim, I was going to get out of here. You're such a queer one. And believe me, I've seen some queer ones but you're the champ. Your face last night."

The smoke wasn't so good now.

"You look big and healthy." She laughed. "And you're good in bed and you don't snore. But you give me the creeps."

The smoke tasted foul.

"You move around like a damned tormented tom-cat and your eyes aren't right. You're just about perfect. And you're just about horrible. And last night—you prowled around snuffling the air and messing around in that water down at the creek and reading the newspaper."

"Is that all?" I was sitting very close to her. I wanted to hit her in the mouth. But more than that I wanted to hear what she had to say.

She'd flipped her cigarette away and now her chin rested on her forearm and her voice was soft and far-away as if she talked to her arm: "I've had the feeling you were going to kill me. And it's scared the holy hell out of me until now, scared me even more than the thing I was running from when I first met you. When you left this morning I thought I'd get the money and the gun and make some kind of break for it, maybe get down to Cripple Creek and catch me a ride to the Springs and then a bus. I know you're up to something that's no good, whatever it is it's no good for either of us, and you know I know you're up to it. So I put two and two together and the answer was: *he's going to kill me.* And then I thought how silly it'd be for me to run off and stumble around in these rocks and how you'd catch me and that would be it."

"It's a long way back to the plush apartment on Beekman Place," I said.

Her eyes widened slightly. "I got to thinking of

what I've told you, while I was beating on the lid thing of the glove compartment. Then when I got into it and there was only the cigarettes and the folded newspaper I knew it. And all of a sudden I took off my clothes and calmed down nice as you please. Isn't that funny? It always calms me to take off my clothes. Isn't that funny?"

"I'm dying," I said. "I'm convulsed."

"I was calm but I was still scared, until I heard your footsteps coming. In the daylight they make more noise. And when I heard you coming I seemed to get the big picture." She smiled and stretched. "I used to go with a major. He was always talking about the big picture. To him the big picture was his battalion. And I used to know a colonel and he talked about the big picture and to him it was his regiment. And there was a general, a real honest-to-God general who carried a riding whip to bed with him, and the big picture to him was his division. Do I make it clear, Tim? About what is the big picture?"

"You make it clear that your wartime activities were not on the enlisted level."

"Well, the big picture to me is *me*."

"So that's a surprise?"

"So I got it in focus when I heard you coming and it added up to nothing more than a dead minx in the mountains."

"A dead five-hundred-dollar-a-shot minx who once lived at Beekman Place? Who left home with two bags and now has two bags, two very nice ones? Who left

home with two violet eyes and now has two violet eyes—
which I prefer to think are lavender? Who has the very
sniftiest of New York labels in her skirts and blouses?"

"You really did read that paper," she drawled. "I'm
proud of you, sweetie. I thought you were faking and
that you couldn't read a lick."

"I'm no detective," I said, "but if you try to serve
me just one more curve ball I'm going to phone New
York and spill my guts all over the district attorney. If
I'm wrong about you, and I may be, I lose nothing. If
I'm right I get the good homey satisfaction of putting
them on your tail, and no pun intended."

Her mouth shook. I put my hand out and touched
the pony tail of hair and then I closed my fist around it,
gently, not knowing what I was going to do. And somehow the hair came alive in my fist and something
moved up from it into my wrist and along my arm and
into my chest where I really live. "Virginia, I don't want
to kill you." I turned her over off her belly onto her
back and kissed her and her arms came up around my
neck and she was crying against my mouth. Crying
hard and salty. And I was talking, talking more than I
had since I was a kid and telling her things I never
thought I'd tell anybody. About how Jeepie's face
bubbled on top the prison wall in my dreams. And why
it bubbled. And how Jeepie kept going over and over
the plan of the trailer and how sometimes his face
looked like a red well; and the well was never quiet.
And I told her why I fooled around at night snuffling

the air and messing in the creek, how the simple business of space and moving around was a luxury to me and I'd never get halfway enough of it if I lived to be a hundred years. I told her how it'd been spending thirty-four months in the Japanese prison camp on the Island of Luzon, clamped there in the heat and filth with tenthousand others, and how they buried the weak ones alive, some of them who were too weak to work, too weak even to throw off the dirt and sit up in their graves. I told about getting my honorable discharge button and going home and selling office supplies until I blew my cork and landed in Parchman with Jeepie and Thompson and the others, and how at Parchman I'd decided I was through being locked up and through being poor.

Virginia kept on crying.

You read about the therapeutic value of lying on a psychiatrist's couch and spouting your troubles. Let me tell you this. Substituting, for the couch, a young woman who is crying her heart out, is the way it should be done.

I forgot all about how tough I thought I was. I went back to the days when I was a kid with grass stains on my knees and my dad was a country town dentist who used to get drunk and sob and slobber all over me. Because his debts got bigger and bigger and his practice smaller and smaller all the time. He couldn't sob on my mother because she hated the way he smelled. I told Virginia how he used to put his face against his work table and bawl and when he'd raise his head there would be scraps of gold sticking to his cheek, the kind of gold they use to fill teeth, the kind that comes in sheets and you can cut with a scissors. I told her how once my dad and I got drunk together after I got out of the Army and he melted down my honorable discharge button and filled one of my teeth with it and from then on until the day he died we called it my honorable discharge tooth. I didn't blow my lid and go to Parchman until after he died. I yakked and yakked and my idea of pure hell would be to have a movie of all that blubbering played back to me now. Twenty-seven may be too young to die. But it isn't too young to die like a man. And if anybody knew of the night I spent up there in the mountains caterwauling like a sick sheep, I think I'd butt my brains out right now.

We spent three days and nights up in the rocks and then another day and by the fourth night we decided our faces looked much better what with the new suntans and outdoor living. I'd fished the stream and we'd swum a lot in the deep cold water of the pool and eaten bacon and fish and canned creamed corn and beans. The lumps on our faces had gone down a lot and I think the stinging cold water in the pool helped some, too, as well as the whiskyless nights and heavy sunburns.

We drove down into Cripple Creek at eight that fourth night and it was like taking a roller-coaster into the town, riding the clutch most of the way.

The hotel was easy to find. It was pretty much the way Virginia's friend said it was. In the lobby I bought tickets to the melodrama thing, from a sub-villain who was caked with suntan makeup and rouge and who said his name in the melodrama was Dirk Sneathe, and that he wasn't half the beast the main villain was. The sub-villain sat at an old Governor Winthrop desk and he said he always sold tickets until just before the show began down in the Gold Bar. That's what they called the little basement beneath the lobby. The lobby whirled with guests and with flannelly visitors from Colorado Springs. There was a steady cackle of talk of one kind and another about gold mines and various diggings and properties in the area. And after all, that was mainly what I'd come to hear, so I felt good about everything. I wanted to know more about those abandoned shafts, and if they were likely to *remain* abandoned.

Virginia was in fine spirits when we left the lobby and descended the splintery stairs into the Gold Bar room. She was watching the people and holding onto my arm. The bartender wore a phony gay-nineties mustache and a checked vest and he was drunk enough himself to slosh the stuff around generously. Two I.W. Harpers painted the room prettily. I got a kick out of being in a crowd of people who were out to enjoy themselves. There were pictures over the bar of John L. Sullivan and of Gentleman Jim Corbett, both stripped to the waist and wearing the kind of pants you see on tightwire performers and ballet dancers. There were pictures, too, of a number of the old gold mines, and there at the left, almost at the end of the row, was the skinny leaning building I'd found near our camp. It couldn't have been anything else, because at the front edge of the roof some of the boards were fanned up and out like a bat's wing, and the rusted wheel and cable were there, too.

I pointed to it and asked the bartender about it.

He grinned. "That's the old Katie Lewellyn."

I'd heard someone say in the lobby that the Golden Cycle Corporation was reworking the Molly Kathleen and some of the others; that the operators had modern machinery that now made it profitable to process low-grade ore that was worthless before the new machinery was invented. I asked the bartender if anyone planned to go back into the Katie Lewellyn. Virginia looked at me strangely.

"I don't think they'll ever touch her again," the bartender said with thick gaiety, as if he were discussing a woman. "The Katie Lewellyn was never much more than a hole in the ground."

That was fine. Fine. I laughed and turned to Virginia and pulled her against me and she, still watching me in that strange way, pushed me back for an instant, then relaxed into me and giggled. I kissed her and the bartender clapped. When I quit kissing her there was a crowd around us, everybody clapping and smiling, and I guess most of them thought we were newlyweds and that the Colorado air and the bourbon were working on us so hard we couldn't wait. Virginia's wedding ring had a splendid glow to it in the dim light and she was slightly flushed with the excitement. People were introducing themselves to us and the next thing I knew an usher in a checked vest like the bartender's came up to us and handed me two phony mustaches. He showed me how to stick them on. I pasted mine in place and put the other one on Virginia and we laughed and laughed and so did the others.

Almost everybody in the room had on the mustaches and some of them wore papier-mâché derbies, lettered in white: THE GOLD BAR. The audience sat at tables, not in rows of seats, little drinking tables which allowed them to continue buying drinks all through the show.

When the curtain lifted on the melodrama we were sitting at a table with an elderly giant who had fluffy blue-white hair, and a woman about his age, and I presume, their daughter who was something else again. The daughter wore one of those handy-grab blouses and she filled it to bursting and under the table she kept pushing her leg against mine whenever we laughed about anything. And we laughed about everything. The daughter had a good mouth and the kind of ragged white teeth that shone when she laughed. I've always liked teeth like that. And there's nothing I can do about it. I simply like them. So I shoved back against her knee. The world was just too damned dandy.

It got so dandy after a time I began drinking plain ice water and I stuck to it for an hour, all through the part of the show where Simon Hasselberry and Dirk Sneathe strapped Little Nell to the railroad tracks.

Virginia kept on with the double bourbons. This worried me because she was laughing kind of wild and at all the wrong places. We were sitting well back from the stage, but at one point she got up and walked to the footlights, threading her way among the tables, and chunked a bag of popcorn at the villain. She forgot to open the popcorn before she threw it and it knocked the villain's hat off on the floor. He blew her a kiss.

We managed somehow to drive back to the camp and the next morning I drank half that damn creek before my mouth tasted right.

Virginia?

She felt wonderful. She split some canned wieners and fried them with the eggs and made some coffee on our rock stove. We were out of bread and she buttered some soda crackers and toasted them in a tin and they tasted pretty good. By noon we were swimming together in the pool. She was wonderful in the water, almost professionally good, and the water was clear because its bottom was solid rock and there was nothing to stir up and cloud it. It must have been about nine feet deep and cold, achingly cold. It felt so fine to my head I'd take a deep breath and go limp and sink down to the bottom and squat there. From below the surface was a sheet of mercury and then I'd see it break roughly as she kicked against it coming down to me. It was like watching her through a sheet of clean green cellophane. She came and curved around me and slid along my back and shoulders. A futuristic kind of love. Love with all the heat taken out of it.

We bundled up in the bag in the shade of the baby cliff in the camp and dozed and kissed and struggled around until dusk. And then we did some absolute sleeping and when I opened my eyes it was night. A million stars, a quadrillion stars, blinking in the wind.

"Virginia?"

"Mm-mmmm."

"Virginia!"

"What, Tim?"

"I don't know too much about loving, honestly loving, but I think I love you."

"You're drunk, Tim, drunk on sunshine and exercise and having a woman all to yourself."

"No. I feel funny about you."

"Then you're crazy."

"Of course, but that has nothing to do with it. I want to make you happy, so I guess I love you."

"Tim, you'll never make anybody happy." She kissed me very softly. "Not permanently happy, I mean. All your love is where it's easy to get at and easy to lose." She kissed me more firmly, knowingly.

"That's bad?"

She rolled against me and I could feel the long smooth sliding of her body then and smell the baby-smell that was there and yet wasn't there. "It's good. You're a good man, Tim, and there aren't many good men left."

Some time later, quite some time later, I told her about the plan, all about what I meant to do in Denver and why; and how the old Katie Lewellyn fitted into the tail end of the scheme, how it added the final polishing touch to Jeepie's grand strategy. As I talked she held me tighter and tighter.

~§~

I'm telling this the way I remember it, and I explained to you before that some of the things that come back to me are little things that stick out of the story like sore thumbs and don't serve any useful purpose. I'm trying to keep it true to life and real life is not a series of nice interlocking ripples graded for size and fitting into a pattern that can be called off like your ABC's. It's a bunch of foolish tiny things that don't add one way or the other, except that they happened and passed the time.

And maybe that will explain the way I'm going to start this next part about when we reached Denver.

Part III

Chapter Five

AFTER WE LEFT THE CAR in the parking lot in Denver and started reading the classified and looking for a house, we were standing on the corner waiting for a bus. The only other people waiting were a young woman and a boy. She kept patting his clothes straight and pulling him away from the curb as if he were her son.

"You know who made me?" the boy asked me.

I told him I didn't know.

"God made me, and all things, for His own glory." His mother tugged at him, smiling apologetically at Virginia and me.

"Don't jerk me around," he said. "God made all things. And once God went fishing. Jesus told him to go out to a deep hole and to get everybody in the boat so they wouldn't get their feet wet from the water. That day when Jesus went home there wasn't anything for lunch and He went to the grocery and there still wasn't anything."

"Eddie, stop it," his mother said. Then to us: "I've been sending him to Bible school to get him out of the house. I'm afraid he's mixed up. He's only four."

Eddie blinked coolly. "Jesus went to God and said he wanted to have something to eat, for His own glory."

The mother laughed nervously and Virginia laughed, too. The bus came and the boy waved at it and said, "Here comes the bus driver for his own glory."

After we were on the bus I heard Eddie somewhere behind us, still talking: "Then Jesus came back on land and made the blind man see. The blind man went to church in bed because his legs wouldn't work until Jesus fixed 'em."

Virginia seemed glum when we crawled off the bus on Colorado Boulevard near the golf-driving range with the big black and red targets in the ten-hundred block. She brightened later after we found the furnished house, a small thing of mouse-colored brick, in a good but not a fancy neighborhood where everybody was out in their yards watering the lawns with sprinklers and hoses. I was used to the Mississippi and Red rivers and rain all the time and down where I come from it is a battle to keep the grass cut as fast as it grows. I'd seen only a few persons standing out in the yard with a hose and it seemed strange to see a whole neighborhood at it at once, but Virginia said it was like that out West.

"The papers are always loaded with stories about reclamation and new dams and things like that and they pray for rain and act downright silly when it comes. They talk all the time about how water is man's best friend and they burn silver iodide day and night."

We were sitting on the brick railing of the front porch and the real estate man was out on the, lawn pulling up the metal sign that said the house was for rent. You could see that each neighbor had a different little system of wiggling the hose or regulating the sprinkler and that these adjustments and manipulations were of grave importance to all of them. There was an old man in a yellow undershirt across the street, giving us the once-over-lightly, but not staring at us.

"They're nuts about water out here," Virginia said. "But every time they go out fishing or swimming their hip boots fill up with water or they swallow too much of it and drown. They love it. But there isn't enough of it for them to ever get used to it."

The old man in the yellow undershirt twisted his hose around so he was watering in our direction. He still wasn't quite staring. Virginia smiled at him and nodded. He jerked the hose and turned around and began watering the other way toward his house.

"He's shy for his age," I said.

I paid the real estate man a month in advance and he said he hoped we liked Milligan Street and that he used to live there himself. He gave the impression I could work my way up to a better street, too, if I stayed on the ball and went to bed early and watered my grass plenty. He gave me his card. This was the second one and I guess he'd forgotten giving me the first one. Real estate men and insurance salesmen generally seem to be loaded with the things, with an unlimited supply of cards, and there's something about the way they hand them to you that makes you take them whether you want them or not. When he was gone I went inside with Virginia and threw the cards in the fireplace.

She said she wanted to take a bath. After she started the water running I went down to the parking lot and got the Packard.

I tipped the attendant a quarter and he looked at me as if no one ever tipped him, holding the quarter in the palm of his hand and not closing his fingers on it.

"Keep it," I said. "For your own glory."

Virginia and I watched the *Denver Post* and the *Rocky Mountain News* for a week without finding the job I wanted, the exact kind of job that would fit into my plan, and in that week we met most of the people in the neighborhood; and just to make it strictly kosher I bought myself a wedding ring, mine of yellow gold, fat and plain and reassuring. The old man in the dirty undershirt across the street came over after about four days and introduced himself and said his name was Damon and that he had a nephew by name of Runyan, and we took him in the kitchen and gave him a drink. He said he knew we were all right when he saw Virginia out in the yard watering the grass, and that anybody who took care of the grass must have a good streak in them. He said his wife had diabetes and the blood wouldn't circulate right in her toes so he did all the house cleaning and cooking and some night we'd have to eat some of his beans, which he cooked with mustard and ketchup and just a dash of chili powder. We never did eat the beans, but like I say, we met him and most of the others and it turned out to be a drinking neighborhood—which helped.

Everybody seemed tickled to death in the nasal twangy way Denver people get tickled, that Virginia and I had been married only a month (that was our story) and when Virginia watered the lawn in a pair of faded denim shorts and the cocoa-colored T-shirt made of toweling, they came out on their front porches in droves. Next door to Mr. Damon was a red-haired Zulu who sat on a striped glider all day long and read paperbacked novels and scratched herself. She had the most hair of any one person I've ever seen if you counted her arms and legs, too. She was married and had a black-eyed baby that was almost hairless and when she came to see us she brought the baby along. I don't know her name and never did; but I know the way she loved her baby was good to see and her husband, who was on the road most of the time, looked fat and happy.

It was a sane and fairly respectable neighborhood for the most part, except for a pale young man with oily fair hair who lived on the same side of the street we did, four houses down. The Zulu said when he got off work he would pull his clothes off and sit in a Morris chair in the living room and when anybody rang the door-bell he would get up and walk to the door without putting on his pants. We never met him.

Next door, on our right, was a Mrs. Mooney, who liked flowers, and who had a married daughter in Georgia, married to an infantry officer at Fort Benning. On our left were the Massengales, who had a two-year-old granddaughter whose head was slick as an onion, and they talked most of the time about whether the child would grow hair. Virginia said it seemed a shame that the Zulu across the street couldn't divvy up with the bald child, share "all those shockingly active follicles" with the baby.

Across the street next door to Mr. Damon, on his right, was a red brick house. There was a long, lanky girl, I guess about nineteen, who came out of the house in the late afternoons and watered the lawn and sometimes mowed it. I never saw anyone else there at all. She was strong and quick and deeply tanned and she wore shorts. When she pushed the mower you could see the bronzed muscles jump in the backs of her legs. She had the kind of ragged white teeth I like. And she was the only one of the lot Virginia didn't like. Virginia said the lanky girl never smiled or spoke, but she must have smiled some time or other or I wouldn't've seen her teeth. "She's an A-number-one snake," Virginia said.

In Denver you do most of your neighboring in the evening with your garden hose in your hand, and I was right proud of Virginia for thinking to buy a hose. Ours was tan plastic and you could see the water in it and the air bubbles white as snow inside the transparent tube.

Looking back on it, I think we were in the moment the neighbors saw that super-hose. I can still see Virginia out there on the thin green grass, watering, the high-altitude sunlight making silver hyphens of the droplets. The shorts, cuffed and very short, curving against the curves of the legs. The young bride—healthy and conscientious and insatiate.

On Monday of the second week I found the job that fitted into the plan.

The job was important for a number of reasons. Until we laid the chips on the line and pushed the plan into action I wanted to seem as respectable and accounted-for as anyone in the city of Denver. If anyone asked me anything I wanted to be able to say: "I'm Timothy Sunblade and I do thus and such. And I live at so-and-so." If I were picked up on my old record before we got the plan rolling I'd blow my head off. I couldn't stand that. Not now, with most of the ticklish little bugs smoothed out of the plan. There was still the armored car and the buying of the trailer. I had to learn a god-awful lot about armored cars and armored car guards. And I had to buy a trailer, long and wide and very tough.

But, about the job:

It was in a big dusty plant on the south side of town,

a place where they made bodies for sugar-beet trucks. My job was what they call a power-shear operator, working a wide hydraulic blade that chopped sheet metal the way you cut cheese.

The woman who interviewed me and gave me the application blank was also a nurse. I saw blood on one of her thumbs when she handed me the blank to fill out and I asked her about it. She smiled, saying, "Lad lost four fingers downstairs. Really nice fellow."

The application blank was a long drawn-out thing, loaded with personal questions. They wanted to know if you were using Morris-Myers as a steppingstone or if you intended to make it a career. They wanted to know where you worked last (this I faked), your age, marital status if any, diseases you'd suffered and when. And when I'd filled it out I had to go to a medical clinic downtown and see a doctor. He examined me for hernia, piles, and syphilis, looked down my throat and appraised my teeth. The job was little more than that of a common laborer, but you'd have thought I was trying to qualify for the Rangers.

I passed the examination with flying colors and the doctor said I should make a hell of a power-shear operator. He said also that my chest and shoulder development was unusual for such a tall man with such long slim legs. I thanked him. On the hernia test I thought he dragged it out a bit and I got very tired of coughing for him; but I needed the job. And apparently Morris-Myers needed me. When I took the doctor's certificate back to the nurse-secretary she sent me in a room to get my picture taken and they gave me a small square thing with my picture and work number on it. And the name: Timothy Sunblade. I picked that name when I left Parchman, because it is a name that smells of the out of doors.

"You start at seven-thirty in the morning," the woman said. "You need any money for work clothes?"

"No, thanks."

"We can advance it, you know, for overalls or khakis, and gloves and shoes."

"No."

She frowned slightly, scratched her cheek. "You're sure you know what you're getting into."

"You mean about the blade?"

"Yes, the blade. You know it'll take fingers and hands along with the steel."

"I got that impression."

She grinned. "All right. First thing in the morning, before you punch the clock, check out a new tape at the equipment office downstairs. It's to the left of the door as you come into the place. You'll need a tape to measure your cuts."

"My whats?"

"It's a spool tape of spring steel and you hook the metal tip of it on the edge of the sheet and stretch it across to see if you cut the right width and length."

"Oh."

"We've worked Mexicans and Cajuns and college men

and idiots on that power shear," she said. "But I don't mind telling you that you don't look like the kind of man for that kind of job."

As Virginia would have said, the woman was getting tiresome. I was impatient to get back to the house on Milligan and tell Virginia about it. Yet something in the nurse's voice kept me there.

"You don't look soft, but you're just too damned pretty," the nurse said.

"Try me."

"Oh, we're trying you—I told you that."

I had about fifteen hundred dollars in my hip pocket and the rent on the house came to eighty-five a month. Virginia and I had to eat, too. And we didn't know what the trailer would cost. So aside from the business of making me appear respectable and providing me the tools I needed for my get-rich-quick plan, the sixty-dollar-a-week job served more simple needs.

~§~

The first five days were the roughest, getting accustomed to breathing the powdered rust that came up off the sheet metal when you slid it off the dolly onto the cutting table. We handled the metal in sheets that sometimes were more than eighteen feet long and three feet wide. The flat dolly was greasy and when a sheet stuck to it as you were sliding it onto the cutting table you had to grab the end of the sheet and whip it up and down so it bellied in the middle. This broke the grip of the grease. While the sheet of steel was shimmying you started sliding it off the dolly.

The second day Spano grabbed a sheet of the metal and started to whip it up and down this way and the edge of the sheet sliced through the palm of his glove and into the flesh.

Spano had been a shear operator for six years and that is a pretty long time for that kind of work, he said. The foreman, a cheerful but sick-looking little fellow named Brannigan, told me that in six months as Spano's assistant I ought to be able to draw pay as a full-fledged operator instead of a helper and then Spano would get the sack.

I asked Brannigan why he wanted to get rid of Spano. He said, "The goddamn little Chili's got too much on his mind. He's already lost two fingers here and part of another. And he's always forgetting to pull the tape from under the blade of the shear. Stomps down on the foot-control and the blade chops off the tip of his tape. We keep him around, he's going to cost Morris-Myers some real money."

Brannigan said I was different. "You don't have your head crammed with chili powder and trouble at home. You got your mind on your work. I can see that."

"I think I'm going to like it," I lied.

"Sure you will."

Brannigan said he himself started as a power-shear operator and worked up the ladder to foreman and I could do the same if I proved I had the stuff, and he thought I did.

We left it at that.

I couldn't help thinking of Benson, the cockeyed driller down on the Atchafalaya, who said some day I'd work my way up to derrick man. He and Brannigan came out of the same pod. Both had the terrible conceit of little men who through fortune or persistence had landed in positions where there were even littler men for them to boss around. I'm sure it never occurred to either of them that they were stupid.

Spano, on the other hand, had a lot of sense and guts but he didn't give a damn. And he had a sense of humor of a sort. The first day I was on the job he slid a strip of twenty-gauge steel under the shear and motioned me to stomp the foot-control, a long bar which under pressure drops the blade. Once you kick the bar and the blade begins to come down there is no stopping it, no brake of any kind.

"You've got two fingers under the blade," I said. I'd almost stomped the control before I looked and it shook me up.

"I'm your boss, damnit, and I said stomp her!" He looked mad.

"Move your fingers," I said, not budging.

He shook his head, then dropped his own foot against the control, and there was a *wharrump* and I saw the shear crunch down through the two fingers of the cotton-backed glove and through the sheet of steel beneath. When the shear lifted, the fingers weren't there.

Then he removed the glove and I saw the smoothly healed stumps. He leaned back against the cutting table and roared and finally I began laughing with him, but I saw Brannigan watching us from across the shed and I nudged Spano. "To hell with him," Spano said, and kept on laughing until he'd had enough of it.

I think it was Perkerson, the welder, who first told me Brannigan was sleeping with Spano's wife: Anyway, whoever it was that told me said Brannigan was built like a horse and couldn't ever get enough of women and women couldn't get enough of Brannigan; and that it was killing Brannigan, servicing all the ladies and doing his homework, too. He'd been married a long time. And whoever told me about this said that some day Spano was going to kill Brannigan and he hoped it would happen right there in the shop where everybody could see it. Later, I heard more or less the same kind of thing from a half-dozen men in the shop. Wettermark, who worked the bending machine where they bent the steel into nice neat crimps and corners and curves, said Brannigan was always putting Spano on overtime jobs, critical rush work that the front office demanded in a hurry, then sneaking out to Spano's house and climbing into bed. Wettermark said in a way he didn't blame Brannigan because Mrs. Spano was one of those women who was going to run around anyway and if she didn't fool with Brannigan or the milkman, she'd certainly find some punk kid in the neighborhood, and that the story was that after her baby was born she used to go to bed with the Tidy-Didey man who drove the truck that picked up soiled diapers. Wettermark said Spano had prostate trouble and was generally pretty tired, and the tireder Spano got the better it was for Brannigan.

Whether it was the truth or not I felt uneasy whenever Brannigan came to the shear and helped us.

He was a great one for helping you. Especially if you were cutting steel triangles for side braces to be used inside the beds of the beet trucks. He loved to cut the triangles and couldn't resist getting into the act whenever he saw Spano and I had an assignment for two or three hundred of the things. On precision work like this you have to get your fingers jammed under the blade sometimes, set the metal just so, then withdraw the fingers and kick the foot-control.

The shear comes down with a *kerwhang*, like the couplings sound between freight train cars when the engineer throws the train into reverse.

I used to know how many pounds of pressure are behind the shear. But now it's enough to say it'll clip off a rifle barrel without half trying.

And Brannigan, who appeared to love to push his hands beneath the blade, was almost comically proud of those same hands. He never for a minute forgot his gloves, seldom shucked them off even to smoke. And he kept a flesh-colored cream in his locker in the washroom and when he'd cleaned up he made a little rite of rubbing the stuff into the skin of his hands.

Wettermark said when Brannigan got tight he liked to demonstrate his own special system for love-making; that Brannigan said a man who knew his art and who had soft smart hands along with this knowledge, could damned well sleep where he pleased. "Personally, I think he's bluffing about that part of it," Wettermark said. "I've watched him. He used to pick on a fat boy in the woodworking department—after a few beers down at the corner in the evening. And if you ask me, the baboon is a phony."

The shop, except for the noise and the rust in the air, was a lot like a barracks. Too many men under one roof.

But every week I was drawing my check, on the fancy beige watermarked paper bearing the company legend: MORRIS-MYERS: Just One Big Happy Family.

And Virginia and I were getting dug into the neighborhood out on Milligan, going to the Hill Store together for groceries, watering and watering the lawn in the dusk, each night making the traditional Denver mud pie out front of the mousey brick bungalow. Respectability all over the place. We even bought a few sticks of folding porch furniture, the kind that pinches you, so we could sit out front in the cool and smash mosquitoes and swap small talk with the Massengales and with old man Damon across the street.

The folks in the neighborhood saw me leave early in the morning and come home at five. And those who cared to look saw Virginia kissing me off at the door,

Virginia in a flowered cotton dress, Virginia in her shorts, Virginia in a black-and-turquoise housecoat. Virginia in a bored rage: "Damn you, Tim, I'm not taking much more of this." And: "Plan or no plan, I'm not going to squat here in this thus and such and scrape the mildew off me." And: "When for God's sake do we do what we *came* for?" And sometimes it was simply a string of filth, whispered in those wonderfully cultured tones, the vowels of the four-letter words trimmed and softened expensively. Whispered, always whispered smilingly at the door.

I believe I'd known it would be this way. But I was depending on her selfishness, her greed, and the threat of the phone call to the district attorney in New York. One night when she was about six highballs off her guard she had flatly admitted the New York mess and her part in it. I figured these things would be bigger than the impatience.

And sometimes she was wonderful.

She cheered up after I bought the trailer.

We'd been there a little less than six weeks before I found what we needed, a homely dented thing, wide in the beam and square as a box in the rear.

The used-trailer salesman said some guy had built it with his own hands, of cypress and scrap iron, and that barring a wreck or fire it would last forever.

I hitched the Packard to it and, Virginia with me, towed it out to Morris-Myers and parked it in a field north of the shop. Virginia stayed in the car and I went in the plant and got Brannigan and brought him out to the trailer and told him what I needed; how I wanted the rear wall cut out and braced and strengthened with steel I-beams, the beams covered then with sheet iron. Then the whole thing replaced, with a strong hinging system that would allow us to drop it down and use it as a ramp when we wished to take furniture into the trailer.

"You want a kind of drawbridge," Brannigan said, licking his lips and looking straight at Virginia.

"Yes."

Virginia smiled. "You see, Mr. Brannigan, we want to be able to move a huge custom-built divan into it. The door's much too small for that."

"Call me Mike," Brannigan said, giving it the classic inflection.

"Tim and I both love monstrous furniture," Virginia said. She dropped her eyes. "And we want a whale of a bed in the trailer."

I explained to him, too, that since Virginia and I hoped to vacation in Arizona when I became eligible for vacation next year, we thought it would be fine to have a rear wall that simply folded down and opened the entire end of the trailer to whatever breezes there were. "I could cut some of the stuff on the shear. And Wettermark would bend the beams for me from that outsize stock in the yard. Anyway, it's pretty tricky, the whole thing, and I wanted to see what you thought about it."

Brannigan glanced at Virginia. He loved to be asked what he thought about it. Especially if it was sheet metal and was tricky. "Oh, we can swing it, Tim, a dab here and a dab there. On our own time of course."

Virginia bit her lip worriedly. "Mr. Brannigan, will it cost us too awfully much, for the materials?"

"Call me Mike," Brannigan said. When he latched onto a good fresh line he didn't like to turn it loose, and you could tell this had proved a good one for Brannigan. He said it as if it was brand new, as if it sizzled against his teeth. And maybe it did.

Virginia smoothed her hips. "Mike," she said.

"The ramp," Brannigan said, "won't cost you a red cent."

This was on a Friday. I had Fridays and Sundays off. The Sundays were no good. On my next Friday I put on my best suit, a very conservative black knit tie, and headed downtown early, leaving Virginia asleep. I reached the Trimble National Bank on Hardy Street around nine o'clock and I stood there in the sunshine, leaning against the red marble wall near the entrance, smoking and sorting out my thoughts and waiting, the money for the deposit in my pocket, folded hard against my hip so I could feel it when I pressed against the wall. The trailer had cost me only seven hundred and that left me with another seven C's, all that remained of what I'd had when I left Krotz Springs. I planned to visit the bank regularly. To make modest but periodic deposits in a savings account. To get me a savings passbook. Then if anyone asked me why I found it so nice out front of the Trimble National I'd fish out my Morris-Myers card with my work number and picture on it. And I'd come up with the savings pass book and I'd be indignant as hell. After all, when a man gets down to the bank early he's got to wait for it to open. And the best place to wait is at the door. And if it's the same door the armored car guards use when they make their morning call with the money they collected from depositors after banking hours the preceding day, well, it's no fault of mine, is it?

And you show me the man who's never goggled at an armored car and I'll show you a freak of nature.

Chapter Six

THE ARMORED CAR BOYS arrived at a quarter of ten. The number of their car was "12," painted in five-inch numerals, in white, in a metal plate on the side of the car. That was important to me on this my first day as a student of armored cars. Jeepie had said: "It doesn't do any good to study one car and then another and another. You've got to watch one of them over and over. Get to know the driver and the custodian, the punk who sits in back with the money. Get to know everything about them, figure their weaknesses and habits. Don't forget that any time there's a successful bank robbery or armored car job, it's because of some human failure. Any time a thing depends on manpower someone's going to flub the dub, and all you have to do is keep your eyes peeled and wait. The waiting is the hardest part. And the biggest. But it pays. You wait long enough and either the driver or the custodian is going to forget the rules laid down by the company for taking care of that money. The supervisor can't be everywhere at once. He has too many cars under his command. And some time, some place, if you stick with the same little steel turtle, either the driver or the custodian is going to take what he thinks is a short cut in procedure. Then in time, if the boss doesn't catch him, he's going to take a short cut on a short cut. That's when he rips his pants. That's when you make your move. You've rehearsed it in your head a thousand times by then. For a quarter-million dollars you can do a lot of rehearsing. Your target's perfect. What could be more perfect than an armored car? It's stinking with money and it's got wheels on it. The getaway and the haul are all wrapped up in one package. If you play it cool."

The driver was a young fellow, short and heavy in the shoulders. He had a football walk and big hands for his size and you got the idea he could use the gun on his hip.

He came out of the cab and slammed the door behind him, strutted back to the rear of the car, and the custodian opened the door from inside and shoved out two canvas sacks. The sacks were heavy, with brass grommets and a draw-cord around the tops of them. The driver, one sack hanging from each hand, strutted to the swinging glass doors and pushed inside with his shoulder. I saw someone in there unlock the second set of doors and he went on in. All this time the custodian of the armored car peeked out through a slit on the side of the car, keeping the driver covered. That was all right, too. The plan included disposal of old Peeping Tom.

I couldn't see him very well. And I didn't want him to get too careful a look at me either now or in the days to come. So I went inside and opened the savings account, and by the time I was finished giving Trimble National my five bucks, Car No. 12 was gone.

I picked it up fifteen minutes after I came out of the bank. It was three blocks east, on Morgan, collecting deposits in an office building. I spent the rest of my day tailing it, making mental notes of the various stops along the route. They have routes just like laundry trucks. Making certain stops at certain places as near on schedule as possible. They collect wads of soiled money from doctors, dentists, shoe stores, and every kind of little operator, as well as the big department stores and movies and chain groceries. Each depositor makes out a little slip with his bundle of dirty money and checks, listing say twenty tens, thirty fives, and so on, instead of four T-shirts and five pairs of drawers and six handkerchiefs. And whenever the depositor wishes he can come down to the bank and get fresh sharp-edged money for the other, as long as he brings along his receipt from the armored car man.

I didn't want clean money.

For me, the dirtier the better. I wanted it in medium-sized bills and good and limp and unidentifiable.

Jeepie had always talked about knocking off the armored car guards as they came to the bank with a crisp load of fresh money from Federal reserve, money so clean it cricked and crackled in the sack. The trouble with that part of his figuring, I thought, was that Federal reserve shipments are listed serially. Every serial number on every spick-and-span bill. Come time to spend it and you're in a sweat. Once I had the money, I wanted to relax and enjoy it.

In a town the size of Denver a Federal reserve shipment of $400,000 to $600,000 is not unreasonable to expect. But on the other hand, collections in cash from depositors might reach $150,000 or more in a single day, and that's a lot of money for a fellow who worked his way through school ghostwriting themes and sweeping out dormitories and serving tables in the fraternity houses for the kids in the three-dollar socks and the Harris tweed jackets. I remember the day one of the boys let me smell his jacket after I'd said I liked it. He said Harris tweed had a special smell and that I ought to know that smell in case I ever got around to Harris tweed. You could tell he didn't think I'd get around to it, but that, after all, democracy produced some strange kittens, and in any event a little knowledge of the better things couldn't do me any harm. I'd come a long way since school days. Now instead of smelling Harris tweed I was sniffing around armored cars.

It was after six when the armored car finished its rounds.

The last stop was the one that interested me most. It was near the State Capitol and the driver went into a three-storied building and was gone almost twenty minutes making his collection and signing, I guess, a lot of papers. Maybe there was some counting to do, too. He didn't hang around on the first floor, but walked straight to the ancient birdcage elevator and was gone. That part was fine, too.

I'd parked the Packard directly across the street. When the driver was gone I saw the rear door of the armored car open just a crack. And an old fellow, dressed in powder-blue serge like the driver and wearing the snug leather-visored cap, pushed it open a little wider and leaned out. He dropped what looked to be a glob of glass onto the street, then popped back inside his steel nest and clanged the door shut.

When they'd gone I skipped across the street and picked up the thing he'd dropped. It was a neatly squared chewing gum package, the cellophane still shining on it, almost intact. I straightened it out and inside were the five empty wrappers of the sticks, each complete, the pink inner paper folded and returned to its outer slot. Old Peeping Tom was fastidious.

Five blocks down the street I spotted them and cruised along behind them, keeping three or four cars between us, until I saw them turn into their barn.

When I got home Virginia was drunk as a lord.

What was worse, she was out on the front lawn watering the trees. That's right, the trees. She stood in the middle of the yard, wobbling around on those lovely legs, and squirting water up into the leaves of the three old elm trees.

I rolled up the windows of the Packard. The water was coming down on the roof of it from the leaves. I got out fast and moved around the back of the car to her. Out of the side of my eye I saw Damon across the street and he had his own hose going over there. The Massengales were on their front porch, clucking softly the way old people do at dusk. Diagonally across the street the tall girl with the sunburned brown hair was doing something with a lawn mower. I knew all of them were watching Virginia and me.

Virginia said, "The leaves, nobody ever thinks of the poor damned leaves."

"Baby, don't you think you've soaked them enough?" Now the water was frothing down the trunks of the elms, foaming on the rough bark.

"Don't 'baby' me, you sheer-power operator."

"Power-shear, dear."

She wheeled and turned the hose against the front of my best suit, then against my chest, so that the conservative black knit tie leaped sideways. I heard old man Damon begin crowing across the street and when I looked up he clipped it off and took a new grip on his hose, turning his back to me.

"Virginia."

She played the hose over the legs of my pants. "Just stand real still and soak it in and grow and grow and grow," she said. "Grow, damn you. For your own glory."

The Massengales were silent behind the thin screen of the shrubs between our houses. The tall girl had forgotten her lawn mower and was staring I noticed for the first time that the Zulu, to the left of Mr. Damon's place, was in the striped glider on her front porch, her head hidden behind a paper-backed book. With everybody looking and listening I did the only thing I could do. I took the hose from her, turned it off, and went on in the house and changed clothes. I could still see Old Man Damon grinning, the long custard-colored teeth matching the undershirt.

When she came in I was in the living room reading the morning copy of the *Rocky Mountain News*. She took it out of my hands and threw it in the fireplace, and said, "Well, let's brush our teeth and go to bed. Or maybe we could bathe. I bought some red soap. It should be exciting, Tim, old boy."

"Cut it out."

"We can lie in bed and look out the back window." She plumped down on the couch. The decorative fringe of twisted strings on the bottom edge of the couch jiggled. I remember those twisted strings. They were chartreuse. In every Denver furniture-store window there were couches with these strings hanging from them. And I've always wondered since if they were peculiar to the town or the times.

"Virginia," I said, "I don't like the waiting any more

than you like it."

She wasn't listening. She began humming our tender, haunting honeymoon song: "If You've Got the Money, Honey, I've Got the Time." More than ever before she sounded as if she meant it, and even though I'd drilled her on the plan from start to finish I had the feeling now that maybe Virginia didn't want to wait, that maybe the heat in New York had cooled out enough to allow her back in the luscious old circuit there. But now I couldn't give her any choice. She had to stick. She was in too deep with me.

She went into the kitchen and mixed a strong drink. It was almost red with bourbon. She brought it back to the couch and sat down and there was the business of the fringes jiggling all over again. Then after a time she began talking: "Tim, don't ever be a gentleman again. Like you were out in the yard when I turned the hose on you. It made me want to puke to see you standing there dripping and grinning at me as if I'd done you a favor. For God's sake don't turn into a gentleman on me."

"Don't worry about it," I said. "And, honey, aren't you leaning a little heavy on the sauce? I thought you were the big contrast kid. Once you told me drinking was like loving, you had to do without it a while before it meant anything."

She giggled. "Did I really say that?"

"You really said that."

"But about the gentleman thing." She waved her

glass. "I want to make it plain as the nose on your face. I can stand anything in the book but gentlemen. Because I've spent a lot of time, too much time with them, and I know why gentlemen are what they are. They decide to be that way after they've tried all the real things and flopped at them. They've flopped at women. They've flopped at standing up on their hind legs and acting like men. So they become gentlemen. They've flopped at being individuals. So they say to themselves one fine morning: 'What can I be that's no trouble at all and that doesn't amount to a damned thing, but yet will make everyone look up to me?' The answer's simple. Be a gentleman. Take life flat on your back, cry in private, and then in a well-modulated voice."

I lit a cigarette and blew the smoke against the palm of my hand, watching it flatten and spread in the lamplight. I didn't say anything.

"A gentleman is a door mat with all the scratch gone from it," Virginia snapped. "Look 'em over sometimes. They even wear the kind of clothes that fit being a door mat: fuzzy."

I grinned. This brought to mind the Harris tweed. There was no doubt my woman knew about Harris tweed.

She set her drink on the floor and came off the couch, all in one boneless long movement, and then she was kissing me and I thought she was going to jerk every stitch of hair out of my head. I picked her up and carried her through the dining room and then through the dark hall that led to the back bedroom, the toes of her sandals rustling against the wallpaper in the hall.

I threw her on the bed and she smiled up at me. For the next three hours I applied myself to proving I hadn't become, and wouldn't become, a gentleman.

Chapter Seven

BRANNIGAN GAVE SPANO AND ME a worksheet that called for six hundred of the iron triangles. That's the way the morning began, very calmly, with the worksheet clipped up high on the machine where we could study it and keep track of the count. As I remember it Brannigan wanted two hundred triangles cut to one specification and the rest cut to another, because although all of them would be welded into a truck body as braces, some had to be stronger than others. And four of them were to be used in the rear wall of my own trailer, Brannigan said, winking. "You've been a good boy, Tim. It's the least I can do for you to do the job right. That thing's going to be strong as a vault door."

He'd taken over the project of the trailer wall as I'd hoped he would and, thorough workman that he was, had become so interested in it he wouldn't let anyone else touch it. The four braces in the corners were the final pieces. And the drawbridge wall fitted so neatly in the tail end of the trailer you couldn't tell it was hinged along the bottom edge.

Anyway Spano and I started cutting out the triangles on the power shear, first cutting squares, then cutting diagonally across each square so that it made two triangles. Each time we did this one triangle fell behind the machine, on the far side of the blade. As Spano's helper it was my job to go around back now and then and stack them evenly on a low wooden dolly. It was close to lunch time when I heard Brannigan talking with Spano in front of the machine. Brannigan must have put his tape to some of the finished pieces up there. "I tell you they're a sixty-second off at the base."

I heard Spano's tape tinkle against a piece of metal. "The hell they are."

Then I heard the steel tape whir as he pushed it back in its spool, and he said to Brannigan, "If you can cut them any closer to specifications, you're welcome to it."

They were keeping their voices in pitch with the shop machinery, down low, and sounded friendlier than usual and I didn't pay much attention to it. Brannigan grunted his official foreman-takes-over-from-laborer grunt, and there was the ringing slam of one of the iron squares hitting the work table in front of the blade. I was down on my knees where I could look almost directly up at the cutting edge and I saw the sheet metal slide under the blade and bump against the gauge. Then the sheet was withdrawn and I saw two of Brannigan's gloved fingers under the blade. Just an instant. He was the only one of us who wore gloves with green sueded palms. It was suffocating behind and under the machine. "Your gauge setting's sloppy," Brannigan said to Spano. And Spano said, "I told you to help yourself."

I went back to the stacking job, careful to avoid the raw steel burrs along the edges of the triangles. They'll lance through leather like a scalpel.

Brannigan came around back, cursing under his breath. Without looking right or left he grabbed the handle of the wheel on the gauge, slipped the locking pin clear, and gave it a vicious spin. If it was off, it couldn't have been off that far, but this seemed to make Brannigan feel better. His face relaxed and he took hold of the handle more gently and turned it slowly until he got it where he wanted it. "Five and five sixty-seconds," he sang out.

Spano yawned. You could hear it. "That's where I had it."

Brannigan moved up front again. "Look here, Chili, I've had a bellyful of your mouth."

"And?" Spano said.

"Keep it shut."

"Some day," Spano said softly, "they're going to hitch a battleship onto the island of Ireland and they're going to drag it out in the middle of the ocean and sink it. And then there won't be so much noise in the world."

"I warned you."

"Damn you," Spano said. "Damn you and all the little milky-legged bed-crawling cockroaches like you."

"We'll go to the office when I finish this," Brannigan said coldly. There was the clanking of the sheet metal against the table again as he slid the square across the table, under the blade, and against the gauge-stop behind the blade. The gauge-stop saves work when you're cutting a number of pieces all alike. If it's set right you simply push them through until they bump it, and make your cut there. I crawled out a little more in the clear. When the blade descends there is an iron bar that pushes down behind the machine. It is parallel to the floor and won't hunt you except to bump your head, since it moves only four or five inches, just like the blade. That unbelievable thrusting cut involves a movement of less than a half-foot.

The sweat and rust powder ran down my forehead into my eyes and the gloves were too dirty for me to wipe it off. I wiped my eye on my shoulder and looked up just as the blade sliced into the square of metal Brannigan had pushed through.

I watched it fall against the boards of the dolly, a clean bluish triangle with clean silver edges.

I started to pick it up and place it on the stack with the others and it was then I saw the three glove fingers lying on the new-cut metal. They were made of yellow cotton with red stripes, and of cheap green suedey leather. I don't remember whether Brannigan began screaming the instant the cut was made, but I remember the screaming getting louder and louder as I came around front and that there were three jets of blood coming out of what was left of his right hand. He was bent over, the hand down between his knees, squirting against the greasy floor. Spano leaned back against the work table, his tailbone on the edge of it, smoking. He was watching Brannigan with the faint frown of someone who's just heard a corny joke.

And that's how I became what Brannigan called a full-fledged power-shear operator.

They never were able to prove that Spano deliberately stepped on the foot-control while Brannigan's fingers were beneath the blade. Spano said he stumbled and put his foot down in the wrong place, and after all, that's happened, too.

Spano was fired—for carelessness.

~§~

Perkerson welded the corner braces into the wall of the trailer for me, during Brannigan's convalescence, and that finished the wall except for some rope and pulley work I was able to handle myself, working inside the trailer after hours so I didn't attract much attention. The wall had five metal locking tongues along its top rim that clicked into slots in the edge of the roof when you pushed the wall against it. I think Brannigan was out eight weeks. I quit a week after he came back, telling him that seeing a friend lose his fingers had been too much for me, and that it got worse and worse the more I thought of it.

"You shouldn't take it so hard, Tim," he said. But he sounded pleased. This sallow little Romeo with the sick-cheerful face had done me a favor, and I believe I really did hate to leave. He told me if I ever wanted a job there was one waiting for me at Morris-Myers and that if I was leaving town he wanted to get out and see me and Virginia before we left. I told him fine and that we'd cook up something good and Virginia loved to cook for company and we'd give him a ring sometime. And I thanked him for the work on the trailer and told him to be careful of his stumps and not to get them infected. He said he would be careful and that one of the stumps, it turned out, was long enough and round enough on the end to have interesting possibilities. He held it under my nose. "No matter how old I get this thing'll never go down on me."

I had to check out with the same nurse-secretary who signed me in. She fussed around with some kind of card. "You stuck with it a lot longer than I thought you would."

I told her about Brannigan, loading it with buddy-hood and man's love for man, and the tears came to her eyes.

She asked for the Morris-Myers thing with my picture and work-number on it and when I told her I lost it she said that was all right but the company would have to deduct $1.75 from my final check. That I still haven't figured. But they did deduct it. And I turned in my spool tape and cleaned out my locker downstairs, giving my shoes and gloves and khakis to Perkerson.

On my way home I stopped downtown to see the real estate agent who rented us the place on Milligan. I paid him another month in advance and said my wife and I would likely be moving before the month was up, that she wanted to go down South to some small town and be near her people. He handed me another of his engraved business cards and said it had been a pleasure doing business with us. "But I know how women are—the good ones. Sentimental as the day is long, never like to get too far away from Mamma."

As I've said, I spent all my Fridays tailing armored car number 12, and now I knew a lot about it. But I figured another four weeks, free to spend every day watching, was necessary before we tackled it. That would set the stage for the first week in September. There's no better month on the calendar. For spending money, or for anything.

It was the middle of the afternoon when I got home and I sat in the car a while, looking at the little brick bungalow and thinking how it was the only home of my own I'd ever had. The grass was wet and green. Then I went inside. And guess what—no Virginia.

There are not too many people in Denver, but it

covers a lot of miles and when you are looking for one particular person it is amazing how many folks you find in the bars and nightspots, folks who are not the person you're looking for, and who haven't seen or heard of her or anything like her. And who aren't interested in seeing her. In my mind's eye I could see her propped elegantly on some bar stool getting elegantly drunk, murmuring to some interested stranger about how she was keeping house with this nut who took turns being Jack Dempsey and Lord Fauntleroy and who thought he'd doped a surefire thing for owning his very own private armored car. Full of money. When she drank she didn't care whether secrets kept or not. Or if it was pouring down rain or Sunday. I wanted to kill her. And I think I might have if things had worked out differently.

By midnight I'd combed more restaurants and bars than Duncan Hines covers in a week.

And no Virginia.

From time to time I had a drink and that helped. I remember in one bar down the street from the Denver Post there were six or eight newspapermen at the bar, loading up between editions. You can spot them anywhere. They talk in headlines and they drink gravely and their faces are clean and their fingernails full of carbon. They have many private jokes. They are about the only people I know who are the same out of college as in college, in small towns and big ones. These fellows listened politely when I asked the bartender my stock question. Tall blonde, good shape, very good lips and legs. Drinks whisky neat at times—water chaser. You seen her? Then one of them volunteered the statement that there was no such woman and all the others nodded. "Pretty women do not drink whisky neat," he said. "They defile it. They perfume it. They dump fruit salad in it." They all nodded again. It was enough to make you sick. My uncle's a newspaperman. All by himself he's enough to make you sick. Here we had five of them.

I sat down next to this oracle of the free press and ordered a double Harper and water. If you want, for purposes of drawing the picture, to consider these fellows the line of a football team—and God knows that is a laugh—the oracle was playing right end. The only empty stool at the bar was to the right of him and this was probably no coincidence. He kept talking to the others. Talking to them in the mirror behind the bar, the way newspapermen do in the movies. Most of them are carrying on terrific love affairs with themselves and when they talk into a mirror they can watch themselves and listen to themselves at the same time. It's the kind of bargain they can't resist. "Women," said the oracle, "are receptacles for man's lust—not for whisky."

This giddy swirl of philosophy brought on an epidemic of nodding along the line.

I sipped my whisky, letting it burn.

They ordered again and apparently forgot about women and receptacles and the oracle yielded the floor amusedly, studying his own amusement in the mirror, to a young redhead with blue pimples and a blue button-down shirt. The young redhead said vexedly— studying his vexation in the mirror—that long fiction was for the birds. "The slick magazines are the thing. You write yourself a novel and you get so many characters in it you can't keep up with them. And you get no money out of it even if you can keep up."

The oracle smiled. He said that he had written no novels, but that once he had written a continued story for the Sunday section of the *Denver Post*. And when his characters kept multiplying like rabbits and he couldn't keep track of them, much less figure out what to do with them, he took them on a weekend cruise off the coast of Miami."

"I don't get it," the redhead with the pimples said. The others shook their heads in unison. They didn't get it either.

"I drowned them," said the oracle. "I drowned all but the two or three I wanted to stay in the story for next Sunday."

They set down their glasses and laughed into the mirror.

They were still laughing when I left the bar, laughing gravely the way newspapermen do in the films, their neckties pulled down just so far, the top buttons of their shirts undone, enjoying the hell out of themselves.

I wanted to find a very fancy receptacle by name of

Virginia.

When I was finished with the chrome and leather places I went down on Larimer, Denver's skid-row, and I hit the little juke joints one by one. Some of the records were so old in these places they were still playing "Bali Hai." All of them smelled of sour beer and worse. Finally I went in a place called the House of Manchu, a combination bar and restaurant where people were eating stringy-looking dishes in booths along the wall and all the help were Filipinos who looked almost black in their white jackets under the blue light. She was sitting at the bar, next to a fat Filipino in a white sharkskin suit. He was running his hand up and down her back as they talked. She wore a light yellow corduroy dress and it was cut down to the small of her back. So there was plenty of space for him to cover. When he tired of one spot he moved on to another, his hand busy as a tarantula in a fly cage. I can't describe the way it made me feel. But I'd never seen anyone else touch her and you can say what you want, but the things you think, and the things you actually see, are altogether different.

I remember grabbing his wrist with my right hand and turning him around to me and how easy the stool revolved with him. He slid off it to his feet, smiling as if he expected me to hook my arm around his waist and swing into a waltz with him. I hit him in the mouth with my left hand. He sat down, his rump wedged between the brass rail and the bar, shaking his head.

"We can't have that in here," the, bartender said.

I jerked Virginia off the stool and started out of the room, walking along the length of the bar toward the door with her. She was snickering. Just before we reached the door a tall heavy man with a scarred chin hanging over a very white collar pushed away from the bar and stood spraddle-legged, facing me and blocking the door. "Felix is my friend," he said. I guess Felix was the Filipino with the tarantula touch.

"Fine," I said, "get out of the way."

He said no, he was going to call the police, and nobody was going to knock Felix around and get away with it. I kicked him where it would do the most good.

We caught a cab down the block and I gave the cabbie our Milligan Street address. The thing in the bar had cooled all the steam out of me. Action does that. It always has, for me. So I had nothing left for Virginia when she kept on laughing in the cab and I'm damned if I didn't laugh with her. I tried not to. But I did anyway.

We were almost home when she said to the cabbie, "Driver, we don't want to go home—run us out to Hazleton, in the four-hundred block, Mamie's Unique Massage Parlor." The cabbie shrugged and made a couple of left turns and we were headed back for town.

I couldn't figure what a massage parlor was doing open this time of night. "Who wants a massage?"

"I'm going to show you a place I used to work."

"Here, you worked here?"

She snuggled against me. "Only a short time."

"I wondered how you knew about the hose and the grass and all."

"That's how."

"But," I said, "I know you about as well as you can know a woman who just popped up out of the carpeting of a hotel."

We stopped in front of a white stucco Spanishy place, one of those narrow high-low apartment buildings, with an orange light in the upstairs windows. I paid the driver, and he said, "Happy massage," and was gone.

We climbed a shallow flight of steps to a landing and a door and Virginia buzzed three times, then three times again. Three more buzzes, then a fast metallic clucking, and Virginia pushed the door inward and we were climbing some more stairs, these carpeted in red and white checks, each check as big as a sandwich and almost as thick. We came out in a parlor. It was done in very good taste except for the orange light, but this seemed a night for odd lights. Pretty soon a matronly looking brunette in a brocaded man's dressing gown came skating out of a door and she and Virginia were hugging and kissing. It was good old *Mamie*. And Virginia I'll be *damned*. And isn't this a *hell* of a note. And Lord how I've wanted to *see* you. And when they were finished with the italics Mamie was shaking hands with me and shaking up some drinks we didn't need.

When we were seated and most of the fizz had died out of the reunion, Mamie rattled her ice, and said with a slow shake of her fresh curls, "Jennie, honey, business is on the bum. It's got to where these college girls and debutantes and even the little high school punkettes are buggering us right out of business."

Virginia was humming between sips of the drink, her eyes laughing, yet sympathetic.

"Speaking of debutantes," Mamie said to me, "Jennie was the only honest to God debutante I ever knew good. The only certified one—"

"Shut up, Mamie," Virginia said. Then: "I'm sorry, darling, but do shut up about that."

Mamie was unoffended. "Use to be that a professsional woman had it made, and you can ask any man and he will tell you his self that a few years ago you didn't find a girl behind every bush, in every park and on all the golf courses, too."

Now Mamie was almost crying. I asked her why it was she listed her place as a massage parlor and she brightened and said it was for two reasons: one, that the kind of people who like massage parlors often like the other also, and then again, it was a good pitch, in case anybody came snooping around wanting to report her to the law. She took us in another room and nipped on a hard white overhead light. There were two painted iron tables covered with starched linen.

"Somebody comes in and we don't like the way he acts, we lay him out on one of the tables and massage his back. O.K. So we're a real massage parlor."

Mamie said that on the other hand some really right fellows saw the Unique Massage Parlor advertised in the yellow pages of the phone book, and they came up to get the kinks out of themselves, and in the process developed other ideas and were taken care of. "There's nothing like a good old-fashioned massage for finding out what's on a man's mind."

She showed us three other rooms, bedrooms with mirrored ceilings. "It's only the furnishings that keep me in business. You got to admit this is better than a sand trap on a golf course."

Virginia clapped her hands and howled.

It was almost daylight when we left there. On the ride home Virginia snuggled up against me and sighed, "You know, Tim, I feel so much better now."

You're probably wondering how I could put up with her. Well, let me really give you something to wonder about. I loved her. Not like up in the rocks outside Cripple Creek when I first told her I did. But with all my heart now, as well as the other way. I hadn't known it or even suspected it until I saw that hand on her back in the House of Manchu.

~§~

I kept tailing Car No. 12 until I knew every bolt and rivet in it, every slit and slot and gun port, every stop on its route and average length of delay at each. I knew the driver well enough to say hello to him and to have him say hello back to me. I knew that every day, at the last stop before the three-story building on Essex near the State Capitol, old Peeping Tom cracked-cracked the back door of the armored car and dropped out the chewing gum wrapper. Just so. Always the same, the door cracking open a little, then him leaning his shoulder into it and withdrawing. Opening the door when he was alone inside there must have been against regulations, but like Jeepie said, any time a thing depends on man power someone is going to flub the dub. The beautiful thing was that Peeping Tom, in there with the green money, lived his life like a clock. He would no more think of dropping that wrapper on some other street or in front of some other building than he would throw packets of twenties out the gun port. I still hadn't got a good look at him or heard his real name. I did know the driver called him Baldy and that he never answered the driver one way or the other and there was no love lost between them.

The custodian is in charge of the car and, I learned, is usually older and with more company seniority than the driver.

There was no doubt that if I was going to be able to take them it would be at the last stop on their route, with the driver upstairs for such a long time. That left only Peeping Tom, the custodian, to handle. He had to be put away very quietly, no flurry at all, and the way an armored car is built would help me there. Once I was inside I thought of using a sap on him, but it was no good, because as long as he was alive I had potential trouble of the worst kind. If he revived after I'd climbed into the driver's seat of Car No. 12, he could open a square panel directly behind the driver's position and get hold of me. Or, if he had a spare gun hidden in the sacks, he might blow me to pieces. The blackjack was out. I had to kill him. And keep him in the back of Car No. 12 until I was rid of it. If I dumped him on the street I wouldn't get past the first stop light.

You can see it for yourself. Alive he was nothing but trouble.

There are several ways to kill quietly and a gun is not one of them. They talk about silencers on guns, but believe me, there is no such thing as a silencer for a .357 Magnum, and even on small-bore weapons such as the pearl-handled .25 automatic I'd given Virginia the night I was sure I loved her, you can't depend on a silencer to work. When the baffles become worn, or if the connection is faulty, you can hear a .25 good and clear. Inside that steel box it might sound like a cannon. The gun, my own because I trussed it, would be used to get me inside the box and once I was in there the gun would be no more helpful than a bathing suit. I thought of using a steel noose to kill him. It's noiseless, but extremely nasty, nastier than a knife. I found in the Pacific when we were on reconnaissance patrol that sometimes a noose runs into all kinds of elbows and wrists when you're trying to get it over the head. In the excitement you may think you have it into the throat and give it a jerk while it's still around the head. And whoever's inside the noose will bawl out fit to wake the dead. There was no other way but the knife and just thinking of it made me sick. It must be a tough knife with a narrow blade and razored down to a shaving edge.

I mentioned the panel between the driver's seat and the back of the car and how you could slide it open. It was about five inches square. My arms were long enough, I knew, to allow me to reach through from the money compartment and flip the inside latch to the door of the driver's cab. So that when I came out and walked around front I could then climb in under the wheel and get rolling. I calculated that from the time the custodian dropped the chewing gum wrapper to the time I was rolling would be less than thirty seconds, leaving me at least fourteen minutes before the driver came down out of the building and began yelling his lungs loose. If the river became confused and wasted a minute or so absorbing the shock of the disappearance of the car, that was even better, and it might go that way. You come down out of the same building for months and months, perhaps years, and see the same car waiting there by the curb. And then one day you come down and it isn't there and it will take you a little time to add and subtract. Even if all you plan to do is scream.

Of course the driver would carry his ignition key to

Car No. 12 up into the building with him.

But bridging the ignition with a piece of wire or a coin is a kid's trick and you probably know how to do it yourself. There are two posts or little bolt-looking things directly behind the keyhole on the dash. If you're using wire you make a wrap around both posts and kick the starter and that's it. With any practice at all it's a four-second job.

As for locating the trailer, the one Brannigan tailored for us, that proved simple. I'd thought of trying to find a quiet alley, which was silly. There are no quiet alleys in Denver, because the garbage men and delivery trucks make speedways of them and the kids somehow manage to play ball in them, fight and race and neck in them. A Denver alley is a fine place to get lost in a crowd. I thought, after discarding the alleys, of some place out on the edge of town, of posting Virginia and the Packard and trailer way out where no one would be likely to think about why she was parked so long. We raked the suburbs and new subdivisions where they were building, but none of it panned out foolproof. And if we had found anything, the distance from town would have been too great, too time-consuming.

Then one afternoon when we were both fed up with cruising and looking, we rolled by this mansion on Gilmore, not more than a dozen blocks from downtown, screened by huge blue spruces and some kind of feathery bushes.

"Look," Virginia said, "some of the windows are broken." I was too disgusted to care. I glanced up and caught a glimpse of ragged glass through the screen of the trees and bushes, just plain broken glass in points. It meant nothing to me.

"Wait a minute." She touched my arm. "A *lot* of those windows are broken."

I told her I didn't have my putty-knife with me, but that tomorrow we'd come back and I'd patch all the windows for the people inside the mansion.

"Tim, don't you know that anyone with money enough to own a house like that wouldn't live in it with the glass out the windows?" She was talking fast, pinching my arm now. "There aren't any people inside, Tim. It's what we've been looking for from the start."

I slammed on the brakes. A boy in a red Pontiac almost crashed us from the rear and when he pulled around us he called me some things. I backed up a hundred feet and there was a driveway of crushed granite and I pulled into it and followed its rising curve over an acre of unkempt lawn. Sure enough, most of the windows were missing. The house was made of slabs of native stone, some of them the size of the Packard, and it had a wide stone veranda around it and a chimney that went up into the trees. The driveway threaded a massive porte-cochere on the right side of the mansion and we pulled into the shade and smoked and talked a long time. Virginia kept saying, "This makes it perfect. Oh, dear God, sweetie, but it's *per-fect*." And it was. Because the driveway didn't double back and come out on the same street where you entered. It kept on beyond the porte-cochere, in a long scalloped swing to the right, and came out between stained concrete pillars on another street. We made the trip from entrance to exit, several times, then drove out to the field near Morris-Myers and hitched onto the trailer and brought it back with us. Virginia was afraid we couldn't angle it between the posts, but I knew we could.

I left her and the trailer and the Packard under the porte-cochere and walked down a few blocks to a filling station, my heart beating against my ribs faster and faster the closer I got to the telephone. I had a hell of a time with the directory, I was so excited, and I remember tearing one of the pages and the way the filling station attendant stared at me. Then the real estate agent's voice, the voice of the man who liked to give away calling cards: "Three-nineteen Duchesne? Just a minute, sir, I can check it for you." He must have been flipping through some kind of book. "No, sir, it isn't even listed. That's the old Goyer place and I wanted to make certain Buddy Goyer hadn't had a change of heart and rented it, or sold it. Old man died not too long ago. Son won't live in it and won't rent it or sell. I guess he just likes to watch it rot."

"How often does he watch it?"

My real estate man laughed his standard real estate laugh. "Goyer, Jr., doesn't even live here anymore."

I wanted to yowl for joy.

Then the real estate man assumed what he must have considered a tone of good natured banter: "I thought you and the Missus were leaving us. Going South. And now you're in the market for six bathrooms and a pool."

I chuckled. That was all he wanted. Only a chuckle, and after all there was nothing wrong with him except the printer turned out those little business cards faster than he could give them away to his clients. "Good-bye, and thanks," I said. When I hung up he was chuckling. Because I had chuckled. If I had cried he'd have cried. He was wonderful for his job.

An hour later we were on our way to Cripple Creek, Packard, trailer, and all for rehearsal.

We made fairly good time considering the drag and the fact I knew next to nothing about pulling a trailer. We wore the long-billed silly-looking caps of straw Virginia had bought for us so we'd look like tourists. She said if we were going to look like tourists we might as well get accustomed to looking silly, because that was the biggest part of it, a kind of over-all silliness. I thought that was pretty smart. And I still do.

The place where we'd turned off into the rocks the first time we made camp was easy to find because of the way the road was gouged out wide in, a kind of half-circle. We pulled the trailer up to our old campsite to get it off the road. And to give us time to check the place out. There had to be some kind of road or path to the abandoned shaft of the Katie Lewellyn mine. Virginia wore rope-soled espadrilles of black canvas and I had on some old tennis shoes that were equally good for climbing the rocks. But near the pool where we'd swum and fished before, she slipped and skinned her shin and she sat down and swore a string of words, some of which I never heard before or since.

But when she was through swearing she was through with all of it and went on with me as if nothing had happened. "Mountain climbing is fine for reducing," she said. "You don't have to diet or sweat or anything so juvenile. You find yourself a sharp rock and scrape off five pounds at one lick."

We climbed the slanting rock beyond the pool where once I'd dried out my socks and shoes, and from where I first saw the outbuilding of the Katie Lewellyn. The wind was dry and cool now and the sun was gone, but just barely, so we had plenty of indirect lighting. We sat and smoked and after a while I stood up and started looking around for the road that had to be there somewhere. I looked until my eyes ached and finally I stooped and got Virginia up on my shoulders, astride the back of my neck.

In a minute or so, she said, "I don't actually see a road. But I see what looks like the edges of where a road ought to be. And even if it isn't, this is a damn fool way to look for a road to the shaft. If it goes to the shaft you ought to start looking for it at the mine."

"Check."

"And the truth is," Virginia said as I set her down on the top of the slanting rock, "you wanted to come up here and kill some time. I feel the same way, but what I want to see is our hollow cooking rock where you used to cremate the eggs."

We went and looked at the hollow rock and the ashes were still in it, protected from the wind there.

Then we went to the shaft and found the road that, of course, had to be there; because any time there is a mine there's got to be a link with a main road or a railroad and there were no rails near the thing, the closest, long unused, being down in town.

The road from the mine shaft was packed hard, and it was clear of boulders, leading almost straight down the slope to the main road that ran from Cripple Creek to Colorado Springs, maybe a half-mile long. Its narrowness worried me, and the fact it was banked high on both sides with drifts of broken stone so that it was really a trench rather than a road. It was a kind of ditch. From the main road to the mine shaft, with no room to turn around when you reached the mine. Beyond the shaft there was a broad clearing, but for our purposes it might as well have been in Egypt. We'd have to bade into the mine road from the main road, and go it in reverse the entire distance.

I explained this to Virginia.

"Pulling a trailer's one thing and backing it's another. In a car when you want to back your tail to the right you cut the wheels to the right. You want to back left, you cut left."

"No kidding," she said.

"Now wait a minute, with a trailer you cut right and the thing behind you backs left. That much I know."

"I bet I can do it," she said.

She had her troubles, but she could do it.

Part IV

Chapter Eight

THE LAST WEEK OF WAITING in Denver was the worst of all. I got into my dreams about Jeepie pretty deep there at the last in the back bedroom of the brick house on Milligan. The dreams hadn't bothered me when I was working at Morris-Myers, maybe because I was too tired nights, and if that's the way of it I'll have to admit that honest labor has its points. I still can't subscribe to it a hundred per cent because my dad was an honest laborer and for forty years he pulled teeth honestly and soberly with his nickel-plated pliers, until he found out he was wasting his time on people who didn't ever intend to pay him. Yes, sir, he was honest as they come, for a long time, and I imagine you could gravel a mile of country road with the unpaid-for teeth he pulled. Of course I don't know how any of it affected his dreams and even at his worst he surely never dreamed anything like Jeepie on the concrete wall, his face welling red and then black, but never spilling a drop of blood on the clean concrete. Jeepie's real voice was slow and low, but in the dreams on the wall it roared louder and louder and more profane. Sometimes it whined like a bomb. Sometimes it didn't come from the wall in the dreams, but from a lonely little plane high in the gray sky, crawling slowly as a sick bug on a dirty ceiling, the voice huge as the plane was tiny. The voice always said about the same thing. What it amounted to when you boil it down and subtract the armored cars and heistman philosophy was: *People are no damned good. Get yours, boy, while there's some left. And get it while you're young enough to live it up.*

But the last night, the night of August thirtieth, I slept like a baby.

When I'd got up the next morning and cleaned my teeth I went in the kitchen, and Virginia had a fine mess of those little pork-link sausages I like. She'd already eaten and she put my eggs on and gave me my coffee, hot and good, the way you can never get it in restaurants or hotels, even the best of them. She gave me the food and sat down across from me. "How you feel, Tim?"

I chewed the toast, smiling at her. "Let's don't talk right now. This is too good to spoil."

"All right."

When I'd finished we went up front and I looked out through the glass in the door and there was Mr.

Damon in his yard, just like any other day. It was strange he could be moving around exactly the same as usual, that the same wife with the same diabetes and the troublesome toes could be waiting inside for him the way she had yesterday. Because I felt so different myself. As if I were charged with cool electricity that washed me down inside and out and at the same time scared me and relieved me. That's fancy as hell, isn't it? But it's fancy because it's so and not because I want to dress it up for you.

We had everything packed except what we'd bought in Denver, that wouldn't fit in the bags and it was in the trunk of the Packard along with the suitcases.

I went out and checked the trunk of the car, looked at the gas and oil gauges and kicked the tires. Old Lady Massengale came out on her porch and said my, wasn't it a nice day and that her granddaughter was going to visit her this afternoon and she'd like us to come over and have some coffee with her and her daughter. She said her husband was downtown at the Legion hall, sounding very proud that her husband had been able to go downtown all by himself. He had a Silver Star medal and a Good Conduct medal in a box with a glass face on it, medals he won as a platoon leader in the first war. The Legion meant a lot to him. And now he was so old his wife was silly with pride over the fact he could find his way downtown. And what had he got out of the years? A bald granddaughter and a railroad pension just big enough to let him sit on his own porch and cluck in the dusk and look at his medals. And, of course, the Legion membership.

We cleaned out the icebox at lunch, eating a scary assortment of pickles and cheese and store-bought cake and milk.

We phoned the real estate man, or rather Virginia did, and told him we were leaving the key in the mailbox, and that someday we hoped to be back in Denver, and so on. And by one o'clock in the afternoon we had the Packard and trailer beneath the porte-cochere of the old Goyer place on Duchesne. By this time I'd lost a lot of that electricity I told you about. Maybe it was the pickles and cake. Maybe it was something else. I only know that my hand shook when I lit Virginia's cigarette and that she looked at me thoughtfully and said, Tim, if it can be done you can do it."

"Thanks."

She grinned. "And it can damned well be done."

I took her handbag from her lap, flipped the tortoise shell latch, and removed her shiny little automatic, the toy I'd given her the night we came home from Mamie's. The gun looked like one of those things at the carnival where you throw hoops and try to win it. It was no longer than my hand and didn't look as if it would kill a flea. That was very funny, as you will see. I thumbed the release of the clip and checked her ammunition, little baby-bullets with coppery noses like costume jewelry. I replaced the full clip and jerked the chromed jacket back to full-cock position, pleased that it slid nicely, pumping a cartridge into the chamber when I let it go. "You ever shoot one of these, baby?"

"No," she said, "but it must be just like pointing your finger."

"That's right, they say that's why in the newspaper when you read about a housewife shooting her man, he generally stays shot. Women don't complicate shooting with a lot of stylized foolishness. The average house-wife has had plenty of practice pointing her finger at her old man when he comes home late nights. Then when she gets really sore at him and points a gun instead of a finger it hits him where it hurts."

"I'm no housewife."

"No, but you've some of the symptoms."

It was comfortable under the porte-cochere and I felt better until later when I got the knife out of the glove compartment. There was an oilstone in there, wrapped in the same cloth with the knife so that they came out together in my hand. I unrolled them from the oily rag and began whetting the blade against the stone. It sounded like when you scrape your fingers on a blackboard.

"That part of it," she said. "I wish there wasn't that part of it."

"You want me to jump in there with him and strangle him with kisses?" All of a sudden I was mad and sick. I loathed the sound of the knife on the oils-tone. I wanted to throw it in her face and get out of the car and start running, anywhere, just running. I wiped the blade and put the stone and rag back in the glove compartment. I got out. I had to. I had to start moving, even though I knew it would be more than three hours before Car No. 12 made its final stop for the day. At least three hours and maybe a little more. Virginia knew the time schedule as well as I. But I turned and walked on down the driveway and out onto the sidewalk without even telling her goodbye. I was going downtown to kill a man who hadn't done a damned thing to me, to kill an old guy whose only fault as far as I knew was throwing chewing gum wrappers in the street. I was going to kill him because I wanted money more than I wanted him to live and I was going to kill him filthily. Or maybe I wasn't. Maybe he was going to kill me and go on the rest of his life with the gum wrappers. I know now that I would have probably backed out of it if it hadn't been for Virginia and the desire to remain a big bad lad in her eyes. Anyway, I didn't want any mushy farewell business with Virginia, no sentimental sendoff. Not for a thing like this. *Goodbye, my darling. Bring back his gullet and bathe in his blood, my darling. As much as you please. You really work too hard and deserve the best.*

~§~

Walking toward the town I thought automatically of how Jeepie would have felt. And then I thought, for the very first time: goddamn Jeepie to hell.

I've thought it a hundred times since, but that was the first time and it shook me up.

I drank a Coke in the Tuscany bar on Fifteenth. It tasted like gasoline. I went out and got a newspaper and came back into the Tuscany and sat in a booth with another Coke and the paper. Waiting. Somehow it got to be three o'clock. I bought myself a double I. W. Harper and water and four o'clock came around faster and then I went outside, walking toward the three-story building on Essex, not fast, but not slow, the whisky glowing just right in me.

Chapter Nine

IF I TRIED TO GIVE you any kind of detailed breakdown on what I did between the time I arrived at the building and the time Car No. 12 clanked to a halt there, I'd be lying. I recall such things as the way the sidewalk gritted under my shoes and how there seemed to be more people swarming in and out of, and along the front of the building than I'd ever seen there before. I recall that the day was bastardly hot for the first of September a mile above sea-level and that a faded woman in what looked like an Eisenhower jacket kept coming back again and again trying to sell me a red paper poppy with a wire stem. I didn't think about anything for any length of time, Virginia, the money, or the woman with the poppies.

Car No. 12 was suddenly there and I was moving around the back of it and the driver was upstairs.

I was wearing a kind of uniform that wasn't a uniform

that I'd bought at Dave Cook's sporting goods a week ago, a thing with powder-blue pants and shirt of worsted wool. It was about the color of the guards' uniforms and I wore a poplin zipper-jacket over it, with a knitted band at the waist, loose enough in the chest to cover the shoulder-holstered .357 S & W. All in all I shouldn't have looked too conspicuous lounging back there at the rear-right corner of Car No. 12, waiting for the custodian to crack the iron door and drop his gum wrapper.

I heard him fussing with the lock before I saw him and when the door opened I pushed the gun in through the crack at an upward angle and that was it. The gun was inside. I was outside looking up at the custodian of Car No. 12, looking between his eyes, along the barrel of the gun. I tried to look friendly for the passersby and it wasn't hard to do because the custodian hadn't done anything to me, not anything at all. Now he backed away from the gun, backing and backing until his legs hit a stool and he sat down, not reaching for anything or talking. Then I was inside there with him, pulling the door shut behind me and there was almost room for me to stand straight. I took the knife out of my left pocket with my left hand according to plan and whipped it behind me and thumbed the button in the handle, feeling the click as the seven-inch blade hopped out of the handle. He never moved from the stool when I swapped hands with the gun and the knife and then the blade was into him and I thought I was going to vomit. The blade crunched going in and somehow I'd never thought much one way or the other about bones. You think of shoving a knife into somebody and the picture is all meat and steel, with no bones.

I opened the panel behind the driver's seat and shoved my right arm and part of my shoulder into the opening and found the inner latch of the door of the driver's cab. The handle of the latch was small and bug-shaped like the night latch on the door of a house.

Coming out the back end of the car I jumped and swung the door shut while I was still in the air and it clanged as my feet hit the street. I had his cap on now, the custodian's leather-visored cap and I must have looked very much like an armored car man tending his business. He was bald. In the light of the iron box his head had shone like a pearl, with a lot of pink and blue in it.

In the driver's cab I bridged the ignition switch with a soft thick piece of copper wiring, stomped the starter and pulled away from the curbing. My wrist watch said the entire business cost me only forty seconds and by the time the driver came down and looked around I'd be under the porte-cochere at the Goyer mansion. With luck. With only the weakest kind of luck. Then at the second stoplight I caught the red and a young cop came off the corner curbing or from somewhere and rapped on the glass with his knuckles. My belly hopped up in my chest and froze, like an ice cube goosed from its socket in one of those rubber trays. If I'd had only the money, the fear would have been smaller. But I had the old man back there lying on the canvas sacks by the stool, seven inches of spring-steel in his wishbone. The light turned green and someone honked behind me, but the cop kept hitting harder on the bullet-proof window and yelling and I couldn't hear anything he said. Then I saw he was smiling and I smiled back at him, my lip so dry it hung on my teeth. But the smile was good enough for him and he waved me on. To this day I don't know the score there. Maybe he thought at first I was a buddy. Men with guns are a kind of fraternity, men with guns and uniforms.

The armored car drove like any good truck, sluggish in traffic but manageable. The brakes were fine and the steering stiff but true and everybody gave me plenty of room with those slab iron fenders.

If anybody saw it, Car No. 12, thick with aluminum paint and the sunlight popping off its rivets, must have been a crazy sight rolling into the driveway at the Goyer place. I shoved it in second for the climb to the porte-cochere and the house-trailer was there under the port-cochere, hitched to the Packard, but I couldn't see Virginia. The rear wall or drawbridge was down on the trailer and I rolled right up inside pulling as close to the left inner wall of the trailer as possible. When the nose of the armored car hit the braided rope girdle stretched across the inside of the trailer it pulled the drawbridge up into place with a slam, the rope sliding noiselessly in the pulleys I'd strung and greased. Presto: no drawbridge. Just an innocent rear wall. Slick as a baby's tail. Looking at it from the outside you'd see nothing unusual, because I had painted it a dead salmon like the rest of the surface and had even dented it with a hammer in places.

The only door you'd see would be the two and one-half foot wide side door. It'd never occur to you anybody could squeeze a whole armored car in a slit like that, would it?

Or so I hoped.

I beeped twice gently on the horn of the armored car inside the house-trailer. I heard the engine of the Packard and then its tires biting into the crushed rock of the driveway, and off we went.

God bless Virginia, woman of women, peerless driver of Packards.

~§~

After we'd been rolling a while I got out of the armored car's cab, on the right side, where I'd left almost two feet of space inside the trailer by parking jam against the left inner wall.

I had the custodian's keys and I went around back and unlocked the tail door and climbed in there where he was. And where the money was. Now I got a good look. There was a light in the iron roof and it was fairly strong, hanging inside a metal grill that resembled the blades of an egg beater. We had the Venetian blinds of the trailer down and without the electric light you couldn't've seen your hand before your face. The money-part of Car No. 12 was just a plain cube, except for the stool in the front-left corner and the light. The stool was the spinning kind you see in cheap restaurants, with a disc-seat of wood that had probably been polished by ten or twenty years of rubbing against the seat of the custodian's pants. The wood was worn down so the grain stood out from it, clear as the markings in taffeta. You couldn't look at the custodian's head without looking at the stool and maybe that's why I remember it in exaggerated detail. His neck was crammed sideways between the stool and the partition that separated him from the driver's cab. And it seemed the longer he was dead the balder he looked and the more pearl-like his skull with those pink and blue tones burning in the skin.

The knife in his chest didn't appear a deadly thing. The brown bone handle was neat and dry. He wore it like a stickpin, right through the middle of his black service tie. But I really couldn't look at it for any length of time.

To the right of him, in an untidy mound, were the canvas sacks with the drawstrings and the brass grommets.

I went down on my knees, rocking with the movement of the trailer, and slipped a drawstring loose. There was nothing in the sack but checks, green and yellow ones, some signed on the Trimble National Bank, others on the City National. There were a lot of sacks left and this upset me. I opened another. It was wadded full of checks. No cash. Not any cash at all.

Then I dived into the pile of bags and began tearing at the drawstrings. Checks. More checks. Some of them were pretty big, but I couldn't have bought a cigar with the biggest. The armored car was really rocking around inside the house trailer now and the sweat poured into my eyes and, to make it completely dandy, I was out of cigarettes. I remember sitting back against the wall, holding onto myself and telling myself it wouldn't do any good to blow my cork. Then I blew it, high, wide, and handsome. I laughed. I raved. I punched the canvas sacks with my fists and slung them all over the place, one of them landing atop the bald custodian's head so that he wore it like a gray Tam O'Shanter. Then I jerked the knife out of him. I had to put my foot against his chest to pull it loose from the bone, and when it was free I began slashing at the remaining unopened canvas bags.

Checks. Personal checks.

I was through half the pile of bags before I saw any green. The green of money is like no other green in this world, a dull, careless relaxed green. It was banded in brown currency wrapper, fifty ones. Under it was another sheath of fifty twenties. The rest was checks.

I think I screamed. I stabbed the knife into another sack, slitting downward toward my knee, hard. The blade bit into my knee and the red oozed wetly against the sliced oilcloth and I hardly felt it. Inside this bag was money and nothing but money, twenties and fifties, all in currency wrappers, edges of the bills flush and smooth so you could read the numbers like a book. Fifty bills to a package. Now and then there were a hundred inside a single wrapper, but most often fifty. There was one stack of a hundred hundreds. I kissed it. I slobbered all over it. It was cool, with only the most barely discernible grain and it *shished* when you rubbed it together. Only money really *shishes*. I tore into bag after bag after bag and always there was money, some of it mixed with checks, but it was always there. I felt like kissing the custodian, too. The corners of his purplish old lips were turned up in a little smile as if he were getting his kicks out of it, quietly, but sincerely.

Discounting the checks and totaling up cash alone, there was something under $180,000 in the shipment.

I noticed now that the floor of the armored car was canted down and away from me and I knew Virginia had reached the mountains. I had the money stacked according to the size of the bills. It kept falling over when we hit the bad places in the road. I was soaked with sweat, even the belly of my shorts was glued to me, and I was half nuts with wanting a cigarette, and with wondering if the mountain bumps would drop Car No. 12 right down through the floor of the homemade trailer. Even though the salesman had shown me how the guy who built it used cypress six-by-ones under-neath and had bolted them solid with custom-made washers under the heads of the bolts.

When finally she stopped I had to climb first out of Car No. 12, then out of the side door of the trailer, so she was already on the shoulder of the road waiting for me. The country looked like we were somewhere on the other side of Colorado Springs. Before I could be cer-tain, she grabbed me. I won't say she kissed me. But bit me on the mouth and scratched my arms like a crazy cat and she told me I was wonderful, which was some-thing brand new.

"Now," she said, standing back from me, "put on your tourist's cap with the long bill, and your dark glasses."

I pulled her against me and she sort of shinnied up me without putting her hands on me and without mov-ing her feet, and then we started all over. It was as if she wanted to claw and chew me open and crawl inside me and if you think that's bad, take my word for it, it's good. I said, "It's dark, baby, I don't need the glasses." And she said, "Tourists don't care if it's dark, they always wear smoked glasses." So she hooked them on my nose. She said she wouldn't wear hers because she had to drive. That was all right with me. The girl could drive.

During the rest of the drive she treated me like a husband who's come home from the office after a hard day's work and told his wife about a fine promotion.

She lit cigarettes for me from the dashboard lighter. She played the radio, asking me if I like this program or that one, and did she have it tuned in too loud for me? She patted my leg and when I dozed she took the curves tenderly lest she shake me around. And when she couldn't stand it any longer she asked me how much money was in the armored car. I stretched, yawned, and rubbed the back of my neck: "Eighty-eight thousand, two hundred and twenty-two."

"Exactly?"

"More or less. Give or take a couple of Cadillacs.

"How much more or less?"

I scratched my head. "Oh, five hundred either way. You were rocking me around back there. The counting was kind of slapstick."

"How slapstick?"

"All right, there's a cool eighty-nine grand."

"Oh, Tim, you wonderful bastard."

"The rest of it was in checks."

"You're wonderful."

"Baby," I said, "don't you realize I'd be the first one to know a thing like that?" I stretched again, carefully. You have to guard against crackling when your pockets are padded with C notes. Even old ones. Later I could wad them into the hubcaps of the Packard or let the air out of the spare and stash some of them there. I wondered if she'd felt anything when she was clawing at me.

We spent the night near our old campsite above

Cripple Creek and the first thing I did was change clothes in the dark on the other side of the car and stuff the ones I was wearing in my bag. I locked the suitcase. The rest of the money, the eighty-nine thousand I intended to split with her, was still scattered inside the armored car.

What I wanted to do that night was back the trailer up to the shaft of the abandoned Katie Lewellyn and unhitch it and push the trailer and armored car and dead man over the rim of the shaft in one lump. After we'd cleaned out the rest of the cash. There would be no competent evidence against us if we backed the trailer in there. And without the trailer dragging behind us we'd be hell to catch. What I hadn't figured on, however, was the fact backing a trailer that distance along a road that is really nothing more than a ditch, with stone tailings piled twelve feet high to right and left, is a rough operation in broad daylight. At night it's impossible.

Virginia reminded me.

She said the only thing to do was wait for proper light, goose the trailer along the trench in the dawn hours while the tourists were safe in their rented beds at the Imperial. She said meantime she had something for me. It was Southern Comfort, a sweet syrupy fifth of it, and we sampled and sampled in the moonlight until we were numb as skunks. I took her in and showed her the money and we came out and got even number, although I wouldn't have thought it possible.

Later I remember spreading our sleeping bag in the rocks and stuffing grass and bushes under it for a mattress. While I was doing this Virginia was getting undressed, and when I was finished I looked the place over and couldn't find her. I was as I said in a fine painless trance, but I was aware enough to look in the back of the Packard and check the lock on my suitcase. I began stumbling around calling her, keeping it low, and I went and looked in the bathing pool cut into the rock on the slope, but she wasn't there. I came back and searched dizzily under the trailer, muttering the way drunks do, and then I heard it. A shuffling around inside the trailer. The little tramp had knocked me in the head with her Southern Comfort and now she was in there loading up.

It wasn't easy to get inside now and it was less easy to work my way between the outer wall of the armored car and the inner wall of the trailer until I could get in where the money was. I saw the light inside the armored car, glowing in slitted shapes through the steel. The rustling was louder.

She was sitting on the floor, naked, in a skitter of green bills. Beyond her was the custodian, still simpering in death. She was scooping up handfuls of the green money and dropping it on top of her head so that it came sliding down along the cream-colored hair, slipping down along her shoulders and body. She was making a noise I never heard come out of a human being. It was a scream that was a whisper and a laugh that was a cry. Over and over. The noise and the scooping. The slippery, sliding bills against the rigid body.

She didn't know I was alive.

~§~

I awoke with the moonlight blazing against my face and the first thing I thought about was the custodian. Coming out of a deep sleep and thinking about him, it was stale and unreal and it didn't seem he could possibly be as dead as before. I started to get up and go in there and look at him. I had a sudden feeling he was gone, out walking in the rocks, his pearl pate shining in the moon. Because he hadn't died by degrees like a person on a sickbed and the last time I saw him alive he was strictly alive even if he was scared stiff. The thought of the knife, even now, made me want to be sick and the hangover worked in the same direction. I pushed up on one elbow and started to sit up. But Virginia pulled me down into her. She still thought I was wonderful. I'd been wonderful too many times before we went to sleep and I couldn't have been wonderful again, at that moment, if my life had depended on it. You say my life couldn't've depended on it? Why not? If your life can hang from a chewing gum wrapper it can hang from anything in the book. It can hang from a bullet no bigger than a bean, or from a cigarette smoked in bed, or a bad breakfast that causes the doctor to sew the absorbent cotton inside you. From a slick tire tread or the hiccups or from kissing the wrong woman. Life is a rental proposition with no lease. For everybody, tall and short, muscles and fat, white and yellow, rich and poor. I know that now. And it is good to know at a time like this. But thinking about it that night after the Southern Comfort was no good at all.

"You're wonderful," Virginia said again, pulling my ears, nibbling my throat.

With a woman like Virginia if you can't be wonderful all of a sudden she can make you wonderful again over a period of time. And now she did and I forgot the custodian.

We managed to get out of the sleeping bag at dawn, shivering in the cold as we dressed, but feeling relieved to be getting on with the last of the plan. Virginia was whistling as she climbed beneath the wheel of the Packard.

As I sit here writing about what happened to us and trying to take it right down the line from the bathtub in Krotz Springs to the very end, so much comes back it's hard to pick and choose which parts of it tell the story best. Back at Parchman the two or three fellows closest to me said I had too much imagination of the wrong kind and that I wasted too much time worrying about things I couldn't control. Jeepie said that was why I was always a little bugs the first few days after they let me out of solitary confinement. He said solitary itself was nothing but a room and a cot and you; and the room was a blank to begin with and a blank was comfortable as being asleep or dead. But that if you began filling the room with crazy thoughts you came out of it crazy. Jeepie said perhaps my biggest trouble was I could never forget I'd been to school: "They've taught you that to think is to be smart but my friend there's times when it's smart to be stupid."

But no one's immune to thinking. Try drawing a blank for any length of time, emptying your head of everything and still you land on a color, a shape, a personality, a grievance. I can sit here on this cot in my cell and stare at the plaster wall, go absolutely limp in my head, and the story, the story of Virginia and me is there in the plaster. At night in the dark it unreels very clearly even as I try to suck the darkness into my head hoping to blot the other out of there. Writing it down brings me no relief from thinking, but it does somehow take the curse off the blackest parts of it so that later when they flash on the screen inside me they do not burn me so, and I can say: I admitted I did it. I confessed it on a piece of paper. I never told any of it in the courtroom. I didn't tell it before that when they strapped me over the car and used the burning cigars on me. I didn't say anything. But I've put it all on the paper and the paper under my mattress and while it doesn't get it out of me, it dilutes it.

Now let's dilute the morning we dropped the trailer and Car No. 12 and the custodian into the shaft of the Katie Lewellyn. It can stand some diluting. Because I keep thinking of the custodian down there in the blackness, floating forever, his face bobbling against the slits in the steel wall, waiting for the driver to come out of the building on Essex. And I think of his companion down there. God knows I think of his companion.

It must have been five o'clock when Virginia started backing the trailer from the main road to the square hole in the ground in the shadow of the tall leaning-building.

She had no trouble. It was pure anticlimax. For a while I walked backward behind the trailer and slightly to the left side of dead center, yelling clearance directions.

When the rear of the trailer was within fifteen feet of the hole I sang out for her to halt it there. We could cut it loose, nudge it and let it go. I turned my back on the rear of the trailer and looked at a slant at the far wall of the abandoned shaft. I looked away quickly and, with the image of swirling subterranean waters running cold in my thoughts, I surveyed the height of the piled-rock walls of the road leading to the shaft. With the road walled in except for the final few feet in front of the hole it was a cinch. You could compare it with rolling a billiard ball down a gutter.

The engine of the car idled, then roared, and I twisted around in time to see the rear end of the trailer almost on me, a blur of salmon paint and sheet iron.

I ran sideways until I was able to circle the lip of the shaft and I sat down there, shaking. The door of the car slammed. I heard her feet on the rock, then a long pause, and she came around the corner of the trailer, smiling. The back of the trailer was some three feet from the edge of the hole, but she threaded it cooly, coming to me and sitting beside me. Her eyes were very clear, the whites blue-white as an infant's. She wore a plaid-wool skirt and a cashmere sweater that made the most of her figure. A heartwarming sight. And I knew as well as I knew the smell and taste of her that she had tried to panic me into stumbling into the shaft. I knew it because I had seen her sliding those green bills over her skin, bathing in them, praying to them. What she said now was: "Tim, I thought we ought to get close as possible—cut the chances of snagging on the rocks when we push her."

I watched her and there was nothing in her face but health and sweetness and light. "Sure, Virginia."

"Where'll we go first—to spend our money?"

"Where'd you like?"

"New Orleans."

"Why not?"

"I want to stay at the St. Charles Hotel and sit up there on the balcony of the mezzanine thing and look down through the wrought iron at the Frenchy people."

I smiled, pulling my left elbow into my chest so that I could feel the shape of the gun in its holster. I made it look as if I were scratching. If she wanted to play it girlish, I'd play it boyish. I'd scratch. My gun. The time had come to kill Virginia. It gave me no plea-sure to review my fat-headed softening processes, my love-love-all-over-the-world trend. The wind was cold. My hands trembled as I stood and took her hands and pulled her up against me so that her back was to the shaft. And now I was holding her by the shoulders, our combined shadow black in the sunrise, bending over the edge of the pit and dissolving somewhere in that awfulness.

But I couldn't push her into it—any more than I could have jumped into it.

Later, when we cut the trailer loose and shoved it in, it must have caught on something two or three hundred feet down. There was one soft metallic scream. After that it was quiet as if we'd dropped it in a black velvet sack, except for a dim splash and the tiniest of tinkles. I breathed a great breath of relief. Trying to hide a trailer is pretty much like trying to hide a brick on a ping-pong table. Unless, that is, you find yourself a hole the size of the Katie Lewellyn.

Part V

Chapter 10

I'M NO AUTHORITY ON New Orleans wrought iron, but I can say the French or Spanish or whoever had themselves something when they thought of installing it along the edges of balconies. I found that around the mezzanine of the St. Charles Hotel there were so many differently shaped openings in the railing that you could see almost anyone you wished to watch below in the lobby, without moving from your chair near the rim of the balcony. All you had to do was move your head slightly. And that appealed to me, especially after the evening I'd spotted Clell Dooley down in the lobby. Clell was my good FBI friend who had packed me off to Parchman in the dim days of poverty, packed me off with a sincere little lecture on borrowing other people's automobiles. But he had been checking out at the desk of the hotel when I spied him, so I stayed on, happy in the knowledge his headquarters was in Jackson, not

New Orleans. Now that I was rich I worried a lot more than I had on the Atchafalaya or in Denver or Cripple Creek about someone recognizing me as a fellow wanted at Parchman. I'd grown an Englishy polo-playing mustache and now wore spectacles with more shell rim than glass in them, but I worried. Or let's say I didn't worry more, but that I worried harder, because all my life I'd wanted to live lazily and glossily, and now I had it and didn't want it taken away from me. Before I became rich it was only a matter of hanging onto life, a good, rugged, animalistic, instinctive thing that kept me hard and on my toes. This was different, this petulant, craven business of sweating over my wealth, and over what it was doing to Virginia. Since we had come to New Orleans and begun spending on a fairly fat scale, she wasn't the same girl. She spent much time in bed, and bathing and primping, and every morning there was a gold-toothed woman up in the room messing with Virginia's hair and patting lotion into her chin and such general foolishness. And we'd got in with a nighttime crowd of wealthy youngsters and this crowd was quarterbacked by a brother-sister team whose father owned a salad-dressing factory or something like that. The brother, Eddie Arceneaux, announced at intervals that he was going to seduce Virginia and travel the world with her. And the sister, Loralee, announced after about the same number of cocktails, that she was going to seduce me and make a salad-oil king of me. If you don't find this humorous, I can say only that I didn't either, but in the crowd we'd adopted this was a rousing good joke and everyone laughed about it. They all had money to burn, or, if they didn't, managed to give that impression, and they laughed about everything. I remember they made jokes about such things as incest and sodomy, and their idea of a big night was to taxi down in the French Quarter and giggle at the queers who put on a floor show down there. I'd never thought being rich was anything like that, and still didn't believe it had to be, or else there wouldn't have been the steadfast desire to hang onto my own pile. They worked so hard at being individuals. Eddie wore a green canvas rainhat everywhere he went, even with formal clothes, and he looked like an exhausted cat peering out from under a collard leaf. Loralee did it with bracelets, pounds of them, which dangled and jangled, and with dresses that left her suntanned breasts very much on display. Both she and Eddie were married to somebody or other but, despite the strings of parties, I never saw her husband with her but once and I never saw Eddie's wife at all. The married couples swapped around and played grabby in dark corners and all in all it was enough to make you want to stick your finger down your throat. If you're going to be married, really married under the law, you have no business rolling around that way with all comers. Coming from me that must be hard to swallow, but it's the way I felt. I'd rather kill a man I don't know and who never did anything to me than have my own children know I slept all over town just for the exercise of it. Virginia, of course, took to it like a duck takes to water. In New York she'd had a sustained taste of five-hundred-dollar nights, wealthy men, and top restaurants before she was hounded into flight. And on top of that, according to Mamie, the Unique Massager, Virginia came from quality stock, whatever that is nowadays. Now, when we were down at the yacht basin with the others, she and Eddie had a way of disappearing. At first I didn't think much of it. I was too busy being amazed by myself, at the fact that I could write large checks and hand them to someone and point at what I wanted and get it. My shoes got better and better until they were bench-made ones at sixty dollars a crack, and the bench-made ones never felt as easy as the cheaper ones. I got into cameras, not because I especially liked to take pictures, but because the stainless steel and pebbled leather and gleaming glass looked pretty to me. I started off with an Eastman Medalist, tired of it and bought me a Rolleiflex because I'd heard Life photographers go for it; then I discarded it and paid over four hundred dollars for a thirty-five millimeter Exakta with a 1.2 lens. And so with suits and shirts and ties until I had so much stuff I couldn't concentrate on any of it long enough to enjoy it, so I became sick of all of it. These were the things I thought of as I sat on the mezzanine of the St. Charles and looked down at the lobby through the ironwork, waiting for night. It seems that when you're rich you do a lot of waiting for night, since daylight is neither sophisticated nor secretive and is more or less devoted to perspiring and recovering.

Now Virginia was upstairs with the hairdresser and I sat on the rim of the mezzanine, legs crossed, polishing the heel of my shoe with my thumb and peeking through the decoration below the railing.

Peeking, as a cultural instrument, must have come into its own with invention of the lacework balcony. This not only affords the aforementioned screen for the observer, but allows him such a variety of metal frames for the object of observation as to keep the game fresh. A fat woman in a mustard-colored dress viewed through any one of the four right angles of an iron cross, appears symbolic, dignity in every scallop of powdered flesh, a champion of all fat women who own mustard-colored dresses. But the same women in the same dress, viewed through a series of interlocking circles of iron—the St. Charles offers these, too—appears ludicrous and entangled, drowning in iron ripples.

By moving my head a matter of inches I was able to see her alternately in both the symbolic and drowned shapes and I did this for maybe a minute or two before it struck me that the fat woman looked familiar.

I slid deeper in my chair and studied her through the spaces in a cluster of hand-forged grapes. It was Mrs. McDonald, Lila McDonald, who lived in the corner house next door to us when I was a kid in Masonville. She looked no older or younger, no bigger or smaller, and the little ready-to-cry mouth was the same. She looked more like she used to than she used to, if that makes sense. She stood by the fluted pedestal of a lamp, looking toward the desk, now and then cupping one elbow in a hand and patting her right cheek, as if to say: "Now, now, Lila, don't you cry. George is coming and everything will be all right." And as I remembered George always came and made everything all right, and I wondered how that gray quiet little man had weathered the years with this fat bag of tears in the lobby, and what they were doing here.

I remembered how after my Dad died my mother and Mrs. McDonald were forever crying together. They cried buckets when President Roosevelt died and they liked to go to the movies together and cry with June Allison in those scenes where June thought her man had died or had run off with someone else. If one of them got a bad letter in the mail they'd meet out on the lawn and hug and weep and if George McDonald was home he'd come out and pat them both on the back. Then the two women would go into the McDonald kitchen, or ours, and eat like hogs, syrup and butter and cold biscuits, cold cornbread and mustard greens, washing it down with a whole pot of scalding coffee and talking about what had made them cry. They were in perfect tune, in that they began crying at the same time and stopped at almost the same time. They cried frequently over me and the way I acted when I got out of service. They cried and prayed over the shell splinter in my head that the VA surgeon said would have to stay in there the rest of my life. And at night my mother would come in my room when I got home and cry and cry over the way my breath smelled and over what people were saying about me. But that's all. She never sat down and told me what an ass I was with my money-hunger and my new red-hot war-hero toughness and get-rich-quick plans. She died while I was in Parchman. I was sorry about that. But I still say you can't cry good sense into a kid's head.

Well, Mrs. McDonald had no kids to worry her to death and from the looks of her down there in the lobby she would live on and on until she pickled her cheeks in her own brine.

I started to push my chair back and get up and go to the room and see if the hairdresser had gone. Then I felt a hand on my shoulder and I looked up into the eyes of George McDonald. He was smiling in a way that lit up his worn gray face and in a way nobody had smiled at me in a long time. With his hand still on my shoulder he leaned out over the balcony, and called: "Lila, Lila honey, come on up here."

I froze to my chair.

"I been writing a letter up here," George said, "asking old M.G. if I could stretch my vacation to eight days." He waved toward the writing tables along the wall. "I'm still with Tate-Roberts, son. Seems like that one-week vacation gets shorter every year."

Mrs. McDonald arrived, puffing from the stairs.

"Mother, you remember Kenneth," George McDonald said. "Kenneth McLure."

I got up and shook her hand, feeling as if I were sixteen years old and sixteen feet tall and that everybody in the lobby was staring up at us. Mrs. McDonald said sure she remembered Kenneth. She began dabbing at her eyes with a blue handkerchief. "We've wondered about you," she said. "Everyone asks about you. 'specially Nona. She's a fine girl, Kenneth."

Nona. I'd given Nona my gold football. I'd held her in the swing down the block, on her front porch, back in the days when holding hands was a lovely explosion, when homemade pimiento cheese sandwiches and lemonade were manna from heaven. How many years ago? How many years since those pimiento flavored kisses? And: *I can't marry you, Nona, you or anybody else. We don't want that. We don't want the listless, automatic desire of marriage. This is what we want, baby. Some day I'll come back. Some day. You'll see.*

"She *is* a fine girl," I said to Mrs. McDonald who continued the dabbing with the handkerchief.

"She's working at the phone company now," George said uncomfortably, hesitating. "Bright. That girl's got bright brains."

"Yes." I couldn't listen to much more of it. I felt like taking Mrs. McDonald's handkerchief and squalling into it. And for me, that's something. That's too much. But this dumpy red-eyed woman and the tired little man with the admiring friendly eyes, brought the town of Masonville with them, blotting out the soft music of the public address system in the lobby, melting the worldly people in the lobby. The familiarity of their voices caught hold of something in me, pullingly, unraveling me.

"Mother and I were going down to the drugstore," George said, "to get us something to drink." He said it hopefully, making an invitation of it. He was going to get him a milkshake to celebrate his vacation, to celebrate thirty years at Tate-Roberts. And he wanted me along, because once he'd sold casting rods and plugs to my father, and he'd sold me my first pair of skates in the oily-smelling respectable gloom of Tate-Roberts.

"We'd like you to come see our room, too," George said. "We're not staying here, you know, I just came to use the stationery because St. Charles stationery is nice to get a letter on." He laughed. "And it'll puzzle old M.G."

I made quite a show of writing down their New Orleans address and tucking it into my wallet, and I said I wouldn't be able to go to the drugstore but I would look them up tomorrow for sure.

They believed it.

But hell, I couldn't bother with them, could I. Why I had hand-stitched lapels and a truckload of money in a dozen or more banks and these were the things I wanted. I ate trout amandine at Antoine's whenever I wanted it and I never even thought of pimiento cheese any more, not once in ten years, nor of a swing in the moonlight in Masonville. I had my own private whore, or my own fairly private one, and if I grew tired of her I could always sit at the desk in the salad oil factory. For a while. Until someone tapped me on the shoulder. Until someone reminded me I had standing reservetions at Parchman, and at Denver, too.

But they really believed I'd visit them tomorrow, the McDonalds did.

Chapter Eleven

VIRGINIA WAS IN BED, all frou-froued up in a pink robe with some kind of white fur around the collar. The fur was so silky the air-conditioning made it move. She was eating a thick cube of a kind of candy they call Heavenly Hash in New Orleans, and now and again she took a straight raw sip of bourbon and turned the page of her book. Eddie had told her that bourbon and chocolate were the thing, that the sugar supercharged the alcohol and made you "think prettier."

"We're getting out of here," I said, going on into the bathroom and starting the water in the sunken tub.

"We?" she said.

I came back into the bedroom, slapped the box of candy off the bed, and threw her book in a corner. "Yes, *we*."

"Don't make me laugh."

I bent over and picked up a piece of the candy. It is

a sandwich of slab chocolate and marshmallow filled with chopped almonds. In New Orleans they use almonds in everything but iced tea. I stretched the marshmallow and held it before her face. "You know, you're getting to look like that."

"Tim, what in the name of God's eating you now?" She sat up, fluffing her fur, looking rather fat. "You never had it so good."

I dropped the candy on the rug. "I never wanted it so good." The water in the tub was almost running over when I went back to it, so I stripped down and climbed in and settled down to my chin. I'd always wanted to bathe in a tub like that and to use the little wafers of packaged soap they have in good hotels and to climb out on clean tile and dry myself on an armful of fresh towels. That had been part of the dream. But two months in this tub and I found it meant nothing to me, no more than the Exakta camera and the rest. I thought now of the bath I'd taken in Krotz Springs the night I met Virginia, of the wonderful bath in the old-fashioned tub with the rim of rolled iron.

Without enthusiasm I began sloshing the suds over my shoulders and then I heard voices in the bedroom. Virginia's voice first, then Eddie's. Then Loralee's. They thought it was absolutely cute to drop in without phoning, any time of day or night. Or, at the other end of the scale, to phone they were coming and then not to show. Just to get you out of bed. It was part of being individual, unfettered. "Jennie," Loralee said to Virginia, "someone's been walking around in your candy."

"That's Tim. His feet get tired and he says there's nothing like marching on marshmallows."

Loralee came into the bathroom, her unfettered smile bright and a little drunk. "Hullo, hullo."

I said hello.

It was the first time we'd ever been in a bathroom together and it was the first time she had seen me naked, but none of it dented the salad-oil poise, the money-poise. She came over and got down on her knees by the side of the tub and kissed me and breathed her Martinis in my face.

This done to her satisfaction she arose, locked the bathroom door from the inside, and began slipping out of her clothes. First a broad leather belt of soft brown leather with brass medallions on it. She draped this over the chair in the corner and did something with an invisible zipper at her side and the dress came up and over and down. On the wet floor. She had a nice uncomplicated body if you like them slightly short of leg and full in the thigh. And the skin was unblemished and very tight all over her.

I saw what there was to see and went on soaping myself and looking back at her occasionally to see if I'd missed anything important.

There was no sound from Eddie and Virginia in the bedroom. Loralee's Martini breath expanded in the steam of the bathroom, but it was not a bad smell and I did not want it. How she lived the way she did and yet looked like that, the dark hair snapping with light, the eye limpid, how she could look half-nutty with health, I didn't know and still don't. She was like the pictures of women you see in the breakfast food ads, all energy and pinkness and shining hair, coattails flying. But of course there were no coattails now. Not on Loralee. She came into the tub with one long arching step, a kind of split over the rim, a dancing step. And it was still quiet, too quiet in the bedroom so I decided it made no difference, and when Loralee leaned back toward me and reached for my head I made it easy for her. Considering the topography of a bathroom, even a large expensive one, I made it remarkably easy for her. We must have spent over an hour in the tub. But finally I decided we should have us a look in the bedroom.

It was empty and the candy was still on the floor.

"Eddie's seduced her," Loralee said, jangling her soapy bracelets. "He's seduced her and run off with her."

I poured a three-inch drink and drank it and sat down on the bed. "I don't care if he creams her and serves her with almonds." Loralee poured me another drink. She loved to see people drink. So did Eddie. Next to pouring whisky into themselves they doted on funneling it into other people and telling other people just how it should be drunk and why it should be drunk that certain way and what it did to you if you drank it this way. And what it did if you drank it the wrong way. Loralee came through now: "Two big straight ones with no water are the same as four straight ones water-chased."

She sat in my lap. "You're so soothing, Tim."

What with Loralee's well-earned reputation for nymphomania, I guess I had been rather soothing.

Now that the excitement of having a new woman climb in the bathtub with me was gone, I was just as disgusted as I'd been a while before on the mezzanine. And I was jealous of Eddie and wanted to know where he'd taken Virginia. Loralee kissed me too much, one time too many, and I put the heel of my hand in her face and shoved her over backward and her head hit the rug with a thump, gold bracelets jingling.

When she sat up she had a hunk of Heavenly Hash in her dark brown hair. But the money-poise was with her. She removed the candy, dropped it in a waste-basket, and said, "You're soothing, but you're an awful skunk after you've soothed a girl."

"Get out of here."

"You're a sprinter," Loralee said calmly. "There's nothing so dull as a sprinter." She didn't throw anything or raise her voice. She just walked out, gracefully, looking very healthy.

~§~

Virginia came in about three in the morning, alone, and I was glad she was alone because I didn't want to see Eddie and his green canvas hat. I had our bags packed and I phoned downstairs and told the room clerk to send a boy up for them and for the boy to bring change for a dollar. I was sick of buying smiles from bellhops at a dollar a smile. I'd had it. I was sick of Virginia, too, and of what the money had done to the both of us, changing a tough, elegant adventuress with plenty of guts and imagination into a candy-tonguing country club Cleopatra who nested in bed the whole day long and thought her feet were too damned good to walk on.

She said she wasn't coming with me.

I said I'd kill her, but it lacked conviction, with the soft nausea of the past two greasy high-on-the-hog months behind me. We were no more the same two people who slept in the rocks and counted our dreams than we were guppies. I loved her and was jealous of her and yet I was sick and ashamed of her, and knew she must be of me. I blamed the armored car money for her cheating on me and for my own cheating and for two months of insane buying and laughing. I blamed it for forcing me to snub the McDonalds, for my fear of anyone hearing them call me Kenneth. Heavenly God. I was running from my own name. I was too stinking rich and bloody and scared to listen to my real name. Love or no love I wanted to be rid of Virginia now, but I was scared to give her freedom because I was afraid of her talking. I spent all my time being scared. When a rich man dies it is more complex than when a poor man dies. A rich man doesn't simply quit living. He quits being rich, too. Of course a poor man quits being poor when he dies, but that is not a thing to lament.

"I said I'm not coming," Virginia repeated.

We stood there knee-high in packed bags, striped ones and leather ones, aluminum ones and plastic ones, all of them very costly, and we stared at each other and I wanted to choke her. I wanted to sink my fingers in that fine hotel fat that was just beginning to show around her neck, and to kill her.

I can see now that about the only thing we had remaining in common that night was a mutual pride in the armored car plan, in the way we worked it together, leaving no sloppy traces behind us, no stray ends. There is pride in work well done, even the nastiest of work. The undertaker is as proud of his well done cadaver as is the sculptor of his best piece. We were a team and a fine one and our pride in our own cleverness and courage during the days in Denver and Cripple Creek, that was about all we had left us, in the way of a common ground. We thought we were masterminds. We knew we'd picked the perfect place to bury the custodian and Car No. 12 and the trailer and that without competent evidence on which to work the law would have it tough. Or so we believed then.

When the bellhop knocked on the door Virginia let him in, then she sat in a chair and took off her hat and smoked.

I phoned the garage to have the car out front.

I took the .357 Magnum in my fist, draped my topcoat over arm and fist, and said, "Get up while the getting up's good."

She weighed it a minute, then pushed up out of the chair, put on her hat, and that was the last we ever saw of Room 307 in the St. Charles Hotel in quaint, historic old New Orleans.

There have been times when I have missed things about New Orleans since then, but that room I haven't missed at all, not even now. Another month and I might have been bathing with Eddie, or wearing a green canvas hat.

The soft November breezes off the Gulf of Mexico were pleasant and salty, satisfying without being aggressive like the winds of the mountains, and crammed full of oxygen. The high-altitude Westerners are quick to bray about the tonic effect of their winey air, but you never hear them say a thing about oxygen. About the fact it is nice to have oxygen along with the winey business, and that if your pump leaks that marvelous Western air will kill you. Give me the Southern air. Oxygen is the whole idea of breathing.

Close to the shore, beyond the beach to the right of the highway, the Gulf was the color of dishwater. This faded into a pale crumpled green and amethyst and out farther, to turquoise. The sun lay over sand and water and highway, thick and warm as melted butter, and until I noticed this it hadn't occurred to me how much time we'd killed in the hotel room arguing about leaving.

Virginia wasn't having any of it. No sunshine or oxygen for Virginia.

She hadn't said ten words since we left New Orleans and started the drive along the Gulf. I knew that as long as we had to stick together we might as well try to be friendly and on the stretch of road between New Orleans and Biloxi I told her my home town, Masonville, was beyond Biloxi. Between Biloxi and Mobile. "That's great," she said. "I'm dying to see where you spent your mousehood."

I took the bait. "Mousehood?"

"Yes, where you lived while you were growing up to become a rat."

I was thinking of Nona and the McDonalds now. "I don't know anyone there any more," I said. "Most of my bunch has grown up and moved away, because there's no way to make a living there. The only thing there is a plant where they make prickly-heat powder for babies."

"We'll have to see that, too," Virginia said. And that ended it. I didn't want to stop at Masonville and visit because I didn't feel up to doing any explaining about Virginia and about where I had been and was going. The whole town must have known I did time at Parchman and that I had busted out the night Thompson killed the guard and we hog-tied the other two guards and Jeepie died on the wall. Maybe the McDonalds knew it, too, but they certainly hadn't given any indication of it. They wanted me to drink that milkshake with them. Anyway, Masonville was a dangerous place for me. The law knows that a man in trouble is likely, through an instinctive seeking for familiar surroundings, to head back home. I was headed back—but only to pass through, and I'd work it to pass through at night. I wanted to drive past Nona's house and see the old swing there. Perhaps she'd be sitting in it, Nona would. With someone else, some nice quiet fellow who wasn't afraid of his own name, a fellow whose mother ironed his shirts for him and smelled his breath when he came in late.

We stopped at the Edgewater Beach Hotel and spent the rest of that day and the night (it was Saturday night) there; awoke late the next day and breakfasted in bed. I was hungrier than I'd been since we left Cripple Creek, and I was oddly excited. Virginia remained silent whenever she could, and that was roughly a hundred per cent of the time.

We had a fine lunch of broiled flounder at the Friendship House between Gulfport and Biloxi, and there were wide clean windows around the restaurant so you could see miles of the Gulf, see such a sweep of it that the curve of the earth was plain where the water met the sky, Virginia chewed without relish. She did not look out the picture windows. The distance between Biloxi and Masonville is only forty-two miles and from the Friendship House to Biloxi is half that, and I was busy trying to figure out a way to kill the hours until darkness, so we'd drive through Masonville at night. The excitement remained with me throughout lunch and later, when we walked down on the beach and along the edge of the dead water. There is no surf on the Mississippi part of the Gulf and little water action of any kind except during storms and hurricanes. The white sand was packed down firm and I took my shoes off and suggested that Virginia do it, too, and that we walk down a ways. "I've never been so goddamn sick of anything," she said resignedly, "as I am of you and your outdoors."

She was much sicker of it by the time we returned to the car. The November sun had reddened her face and her eyes were puffy. But don't get me wrong. Virginia was beautiful, even though the time in New Orleans hadn't done anything for her, inside or out. And I knew she was yearning for the yacht basin and for the partying with all those sprightly characters there. Once she'd told me that buddying with the rich made her feel as if her own money were more natural and that she'd always had it and didn't steal it. I told her she didn't have to forget the stealing to feel natural about it, that most of her new friends stole theirs one way or another, or their daddies or grand-daddies did. And I reminded her of what she once said: "There's no bad money." Imagine having to remind her, or having to rationalize money for a woman who once stripped down and bathed buck naked in it. At any rate, she was worn out when we returned to the car, having developed, during her recent New Orleans associations, the idea that exercise consumes intelligence.

We ate supper at the Friendship House, after a brief drive through Biloxi and then back to the restaurant; and I killed an hour or so drinking and putting nickels in a machine in the bar. I remember the machine flashed printed questions on a glass face. If you pressed the numbered button corresponding to the number of the right answer you won some nickels. There was only a second or so to pick the proper answers. I couldn't win. Virginia won five times out of five. When we left the bar, the sky was dark.

Chapter Twelve

AT MASONVILLE I LEFT the highway, turning left into Walnut and north along it through the downtown section under the queer street lights of striped glass, dim and yellow and familiar, like no lights you'll see anywhere else.

I know every lump and bump in Walnut Street, from the highway intersection to Doc Simrall's Drugs at the far end, and I could close my eyes and tell you by the seat of my pants where I was. I turned right at the drugstore. I got a glance of young faces inside in the three varnished booths where once I'd chopped Nona's initials and mine under a bench, cutting the initials blind, just from feel, and telling her they'd always be under the bench. NH—KM. Always there in their secret hard-to-find place, and no matter how many times Doc sandpapered and plastic-wooded the scars on the tables and the tops of the benches he'd never be able to erase the initials of Nona Hickman and Kenneth Mc-Lure.

We left Walnut and three blocks down Sycamore I began straining to see the Hickman place, although I knew it was the last house on the right on the corner of the fourth block. The street light on the corner was the same, of striped glass like the ones in town, the stripes vertical down the sides of the lamp, curving to a point, a dark hub, at the bottom tip where it was loaded with dead moths and night bugs. And Nona's porch and the slatted swing were the same. Except I wasn't on it. And she wasn't there either. I slowed the car to a crawl and circled the block and passed the porch again.

Virginia said, "You in love with that shack?"

I told her to shut up.

We were within three blocks of the Illinois-Central tracks near where North Street runs into West Fourth when I saw the red blinker in the rear-vision mirror and heard the siren begin its long low wailing.

"Tell 'em shut up," Virginia said. "Tell the police to shut up." She began laughing hysterically as the blinker grew bigger behind us and the noise of the siren increased.

I kicked the Packard up to fifty and we whumped up and over the tracks and had covered most of the half block to the intersection when I heard the shot, the sound of glass shattering, and I braked hard, skidding to a stop on the right side of North near the corner, the squad car swerving wide to miss my rear and then coming to a halt on the opposite side of the street. I heard Virginia fumbling in her purse and it seemed a hell of a time to be counting her money or lipsticking herself. I could see the navy-blue uniforms and the shine of their buttons beneath the street light and all of it seemed to be in slow-motion and almost soundless; only a few sounds, little ones—the buttons of my jacket sleeve against the steering wheel, Virginia fumbling in her purse, the muffled slamming of the doors of the squad car, very dim and somehow out of time, as if we were watching a worn-out film and whoever dubbed in the sound track had made a mess of it. Virginia was giggling and that was dim and far away, too, and my mind was racing back and back as I tried to figure how in God's name they spotted me and why they were looking for me and if this had to do with Parchman or with the dead old man in the armored car at the bottom of the Katie Lewellyn. And if Clell Dooley, my good FBI friend, had, after all, managed to pick up a sniff of me in the St. Charles Hotel the day I saw him checking out. The cop nearest me came across the street to my door and the other one remained on the far side of the squad car, his head and shoulders showing above it. The cop at my door was young and blond and confident and he had a pretty nickel-plated gun in his right hand as he opened the door with his left hand. It was a very pretty gun, I remember that, and as he opened the door I said inanely, "What's wrong, officer?" I gave him a puzzled look and said it the same way I would have if he'd caught me speeding.

I remember seeing the glow of a flashlight on the windshield and hearing no noise and he was standing there in the door and then he wasn't. I looked down at my right hand, stunned, halfway expecting to see the .357 Magnum S & W smoking in my fist. But it wasn't there. Then Virginia fired again, past my chest and through the door at the other policeman across the street; out of the corner of my eye I saw the cop across the street rest his forearm against the roof of the squad car. The steel door frame *kerwhanged* near my cheek as he fired, and then I was out of the Packard and running to get it between me and him and hoping Virginia would have sense enough to do something like that.

Just as I got around to the other side, the Packard's engine howled and the wheels clawed into the road and Virginia took it around the corner on two wheels, the rubber screaming as she swung right into West Fourth, leaving me there in the street with the dead blond boy and the other one behind the squad car still shooting. There was a pause and he must have reloaded, and then he came out from behind the squad car yelling and shooting and I raised my gun then and pulled the trigger fast, twice, and he lay down on the road. He didn't fall—he lay down easy, as if he were crawling into bed, first the palms of the hands, then the knees and the rest. I shoved the gun back into the shoulder holster and looked around me. The squad car was parked in front of a white frame house and now I saw a woman and girl come out on the porch and begin yelling. There were houses all along the street but these were the only people in sight and there were no cars.

I began running north on North Street, and when I reached the Illinois-Central tracks I left the street and followed them perhaps a half-mile. It was black along the tracks, and cool. I was going east, out toward the college. My mouth was dry and my throat ached and my old head wound seemed to be doing flip-flops beneath my skull, and I couldn't figure what I should do with the gun. I thought of throwing it into the grassy ditch along the tracks, getting rid of it, but then I thought that would be silly, because when they catch a cop killer they kill him, and I might as well die shooting as arguing or praying. I had no chance of getting outside the town on foot. By this time the sirens were howling all over town, you could hear them, far away and like hornets, but some of them getting closer, closer and louder. Dear Virginia—good and wonderful Virginia. She was a snake, a beautiful snake, but not that big a one. She must have panicked. The wind along the track was black and salty and cold.

I needed a car.

I left the tracks and angled through and across the ditch to a house with a stone chimney and one of those garages that are part of the house. There was a light on in there, only one light in one room, and no sounds as I circled the house. I went into the garage and there was a green Chevrolet, the doors of which were unlocked. But before I could slide onto the seat an overhead light flooded the garage and a big man in brown slacks and a white polo shirt came out from a door in the side of the house.

"What do you want?" he said. "What do you want here?"

I was sorry he had seen me because I didn't want to kill him and my head hurt and I didn't even want to have to think about it. And then it hit me that there was no reason to kill him because the women who had come out on the porch of the white frame house, or rather the woman and the girl, had got a look at me and by now my description was no secret. "Get in there and find you a chair and don't move out of it," I snapped.

"Yes, sir."

"I'm going to watch you through the window a while, and if I see you pick up the phone you're a dead soldier."

"Yes, sir, I won't."

"Now, get."

"Yessir."

The car was no good. If I took it now he'd hear me leave and phone immediately, giving the model, color, and tag number. I wheeled and sprinted out of the garage, curving between it and the house next door as a squad car passed out front, the siren wide open, blinkers burning.

You've never heard a siren until you've heard one looking for you and you alone. Then you really hear it and know what it is and understand that the man who invented it was no man, but a fiend from hell who patched together certain sounds and blends of sounds in a way that would paralyze and sicken. You sit in your living room and hear a siren and it's a small and lonesome thing and all it means to you is that you have to listen until it goes away. But when it is after you, it is the texture of the whole world. You will hear it until you die. It tears the guts out of you like a drill against a nerve and it moves into you and expands. I'm glad I'll never have to listen to another siren. I'm glad no one will ever hunt for me again and that I'm finished with running and hearing them hunt me.

I was walking toward the college, along Oak, when they caught up with me, the lights of the squad car swinging into me from somewhere that I can't remember even though I know this town the way I know my hand. By then I must have been dazed because one of them had the drop on me with a sawed-off shotgun before my eyes were fit for that light, and another was jerking the gun from me.

Then one of them brought his knee up into my groin and I bent over and someone kicked me in the side of the head and said, "You dirty cop-killing rat."

Someone else said, "Why'd you kill them boys?"

I said, "Because they were shooting at me." It didn't matter what I said anyway so there was no use dragging Virginia along for the ride. One of them kicked me or hit me in the side and I went out cold and when I came around I was standing beside the squad car somewhere out in the country and there were three of them there with me. There were some trees, but there was a cleared space, too, between the trees. I didn't know any of them. It was like I'd told Virginia, I'd been away a long time. They unzipped the blue poplin jacket I'd bought for the armored car robbery, shucked it off me, then removed everything else but my socks and shorts. The shorts seemed very white in the dark, shock-ingly white. Then they took them off, too, and spread me backward over the hood of the squad car and began questioning me. They wanted to know who had been with me in the burglary of Clarence Kellam's grocery and who was with me later when the two policemen caught up with me on North Street and I killed them. I told them I didn't know anything about the grocery store burglary and they didn't like my answer. I blacked out again, the pain swimming up through my belly and exploding in my chest.

In a way it was funny.

Virginia and I cruising along so secure in the knowledge we had done a perfect job on the armored car, so smug about our fine engineering and planning, our network of plans within plans and destruction of evidence. Then what happens. We run into a brand new mess, in connection with a burglary here in Masonville, a petty, silly little two-bit job we had nothing to do with. That's why the two policemen had stopped us. They didn't know me at all when they stopped us at the intersection of West Fourth and North and if I'd said I was Tim Sunblade and this was my wife, Virginia, and we were on our vacation, going to Mobile, that might have done it. If only Virginia hadn't started shooting. They didn't give a damn who murdered the custodian of an armored car in Denver, who rolled off with $180,000. They just wanted to find the fellow who swiped thirty-five dollars and a side of bacon from Clarence Kellam's in Masonville, Mississippi, the night of November first, the night of right now.

It certainly had its comic side.

Except that they kept hitting me in the face and ribs and the way I was tied onto the hood of the squad car was not comfortable.

And they had a game. It seems all three of them smoked cigars and in this game they tried to figure out every possible way to use me for an ashtray. Sometimes the cigars went out. But they lighted them again and kept inventing new ways and places to stub out the cigars. They had plenty of matches. I stuck to my story —I knew nothing about the burglary—and it was a true story and they didn't like it, but what they disliked particularly was I had killed two of their buddies, and wouldn't tell who was with me when I did it. It surprised me that I would cover for Virginia. But then, if I'd said a gorgeous blonde was with me, that wouldn't have changed my status as an ash tray because it didn't sound like the truth. You don't think of gorgeous blondes and grocery store robberies at the same time. And, further, she hadn't asked to come to Masonville where we got in all the trouble, she'd wanted to stay with the green canvas hat and the Heavenly Hash. Let her grow fat and spend her money and find her way back to Beekman Place. Again I lost consciousness.

Next time I came around I had all my clothes on and we were pulling up in front of City Hall and there was a crowd of at least five hundred out front, screaming and waving at the squad car. One of the three cigar-smoking policemen said to me, "How'd you feel if we turned our backs on you now and let them tear you limb from limb?"

"I'd rather be an ash tray," I said.

Faces were all around the windows of the squad car. I sat on the back seat between two of the cigar smokers, and the one who had asked me how I felt about the crowd said now: "You're sure you won't tell us who was with you?"

"Sure," I said, "I'll tell you."

He leaned forward. "All right."

"*I was with Lana Turner.*"

Inside the jail, in the basement of City Hall, was worse than the earlier questioning. The mob of townspeople was crammed in the corridor that led from the chief's office past the jail kitchen to the cell block in the rear. Someone in the crowd, no doubt an old school chum of mine, spat in my face. I was taken first to the chief's office and that was bad, because I'd known him from the time I was a baby and he used to fix parking tickets in exchange for Dad's fixing his teeth. The chief used to bring us quail sometimes when he'd been hunting.

"Son," he said, looking around apologetically at the others in the room, apparently feeling he'd made a mistake in calling me son, "the reason the boys are going so hard on you is they think there were others with you and that if we're going to catch 'em we'll do it tonight or not at all."

"That's reasonable," I said.

"I don't want these fellows to hurt you, but you can see how the quicker they get the information, the better it will be all 'round."

"Sure."

"Now don't you want to say something?"

"Yes."

"All right, boy, say it for me."

"Don't your hired monkeys ever run out of cigars?" He winced. "We want to be fair with you, Kenneth, if you'll only talk."

There must have been fifteen city policemen in the chief's office now and three or four state highway patrolmen and a sprinkling of blue-suited, black-shoed men wearing deputy sheriffs' badges, small gold ones, only slightly larger than the shield on a Phi Delta Theta fraternity pin. One of these deputies came forward and said, "Chief, they's no use messing with him and you know it."

Again they pushed me through the crowd in the corridor, this time to the cell block, and we went inside an empty cell and from there on out the things that happened earlier were purely fun. I remember screaming and the screams were falsetto and I wouldn't have known they came out of me except I felt my mouth open, my jaws locked wide, and I felt the vibration of the screaming and the strain on my throat. The clothes came off again and there was much twisting and pinching and bending after they handcuffed me to the footrail of the cot. I'd pass out and come back, on and off like a bad bulb, and each time I came around the cot was bloodier, and once one of the policemen, or deputies or state patrolmen, protested that he didn't like me bleeding all over his handcuffs because they were new and had cost him a lot of money. Finally I told them that when the shooting started I was with a fat red-headed woman and that she weighed around a hundred and seventy pounds and was pregnant with my child. They disliked this story most of all, even more than the Lana Turner one. And they hated the color of the car I gave them. I told them it was yellow. The Packard was black at night, and in daylight it was midnight blue, the kind with silver winking down deep in it underneath the blue.

The next time I came to the handcuffs were gone and I was lying on my back on the cot, alone in the cell, the light off. A drunk was singing in the next cell. I tried to lift my right hand to feel what was left of my face and my arm wouldn't work. I raised the left hand without much trouble and put it against my face and screamed. I must have stuck one of my fingernails into a bad place.

It was quite a homecoming.

~§~

The county attorney's name was Kenneth, just like mine. He was tall and willowy with long flat feet and the kind of cheeks that flash red, then drain pale in a second, as if blood flowed into a plastic disc and out again. I had gone to school with him, traded knives and sucker balls and Holloway suckers of caramel with him. All of this was in his face when he came into the cell and they locked the door behind him and left us alone. "Kenneth, why'd you do it?" he said.

"Kenneth," I said, "I cannot tell a lie. I shot them because I wanted to see their blood squirt."

"Now, Kenneth," he said, frowning, "don't talk like that."

We kept Kennething each other for ten minutes, maybe more, and my face was killing me and my right arm hung down as if there were no bone in it. I was polka-dotted with pain from the cigar burns and the places on my buttocks hurt especially. I Kennethed him and he Kennethed me and we got nowhere, because he wanted what the others wanted, for me to get down on my knees and sob out the whole thing, the color of the getaway car and who I'd been with. The woman and girl in the white frame house on North and Fourth had got a glimpse of the car as it skidded away from the corner, but in the excitement they hadn't paid much attention to it. Or so Kenneth Hawkins, prosecuting attorney for Mulvaney County, Mississippi, told me. Virginia was probably back in New Orleans, bathing with Loralee and Eddie. Maybe they were floating chocolate-marshmallows in the tub. I grinned, but cut it short when it seemed my right cheekbone might fall off in my lap. I didn't want that to happen, because I didn't want to see my right cheekbone any sooner than I had to.

Then the district attorney joined us. I had never seen him before, but his voice and mannerisms were the same as those of the county attorney, only more so, and he brought with him a little recording machine and there was a translucent, slick blue recording disc on its turn table. He was wearing a dark-gray pin-striped double-breasted suit and on the knees of it the stripes were worn off. He wore a shirt with genuine French cuffs and he was so proud of them he kept shooting them out of his jacket sleeves and glancing at them as if they were a perpetual and pleasant surprise to him. He plugged the wire into the light socket and monkeyed with the recording machine. When he was finished he handed me a small microphone, the size of a biscuit, saying, "You'll talk into that."

"Sure."

He flipped a switch and the blue disc began revolving. "O.K." he said, borrowing the mike, and giving it back to me when he was finished: "Start at the beginning and just tell us what happened from the time you hit town until now, tell it in sequence and keep it simple."

"Fine," I said into the mike.

He borrowed it again to say: "And you understand we are offering you no reward, no promises of a softened sentence, nothing."

"Right."

"And," he said into the microphone, "everything you say you will say of your own free will and accord." He handed it back to me hurriedly.

"Yes."

"O.K., let's go with it."

I cleared my throat. "The friendly cow all red and white I love with all my heart . . ."

"You want me to get the cops back in here with you?" he said.

"She gives me milk with all her might to eat with apple tart."

The district attorney snapped the switch on the recording machine and he and the county attorney moved off to the corner of the cell nearest the door, their backs to me, whispering. Kenneth Hawkins kept shaking his head negatively, and the district attorney kept nodding his head up and down, until finally Kenneth Hawkins said in a loud whisper, "Darn it, Ted, if we let them beat him any more they're going to kill him. Moore and O'Malley are dying to get in here and finish him off, and so are all the others. And even if they don't kill him they'll make such a mess of him it'll be all over the county, and that will be great for the defense, won't it?"

The defense? I felt better. I don't think it had occurred to me they would bother with a trial—not until then. I flipped the switch on the microphone. I mooed into the microphone, then hung it on its hook on the side of the portable machine.

They left, taking the machine with them, and Kenneth Hawkins said he would come back soon and bring me some cigarettes and a doctor to look at my arm and face. "You need some attention," he said in his county-attorney voice, making it sound official and immediate and as if he had statistics and various authorities to support his decision.

It must have been ten in the morning.

Virginia had had more than twelve hours to get away. The more my face hurt, the more I wanted her to get away. I lay down and I was dozing when Moore and O'Malley clanged the door behind them. I guess it was Moore and O'Malley because Hawkins said they were the ones who wanted most to finish me off and this pair worked along those lines. They began by playing around with my right arm, the bad one, and that was stupid because it knocked me out and they had to go to a lot of trouble with ice water and ammonia. At noon when the Negro trusty came with the stew and bread on the tray they were still with me. We didn't take any time out for lunch, but one of them drank the water on the tray and it seemed to revive him. When he came back to me he broke the fingers of my left hand, one by one, neatly and with no wasted action, the way you'd snap celery at the table, almost politely. That finished me for the day, but I remember I hung on until he reached my thumb, and I thought as I floated off into the screaming pain and grayness that if I had taken this much of it I could take whatever else there was, without talking, and that when I regained consciousness this time maybe I'd be stronger, strong enough to butt the brains out of my head on the stone walls. Or maybe I could find a way out. Then the grayness settled more firmly about me, I was embedded in it and it was made of whirling knives and strange talk. And in it there was crying, the crying of my mother and of Mrs. McDonald, who wanted to drink a milkshake with me. And my mother was crying harder and harder and saying to Mrs. McDonald: "If the war hadn't hurt Kenneth's head he would be just as nice as anybody, as nice as anybody at all." And Mrs. McDonald said the VA had a new way now to pull shell splinters out of heads that were hurt in the war. Mrs. McDonald said they poured milkshake in the hole and then they packed it with ice. Milkshake. Ice. All through it was this terrible thirst that was also part of the pain, and I heard myself say ringingly, as if I spoke into one end of a tunnel and listened to myself at the other: *My dad used to be a taxpayer here and he helped pay for the pipes for the water, and you better not drink my water. He'll pull every tooth from your head.* And Virginia and Mr. Damon were watering some grass, holding onto the same hose, and Mr. Damon said he had a nephew named Runyan, and with this he laughed and jetted water up into the elm trees, his long custard-colored teeth the same color as his undershirt.

~§~

After they transferred me from the city jail to county jail it was better and a doctor came in daily to look at me and smear zinc oxide on me and check the splints on my fingers. He was a young doctor with the tender unmarked hands of a woman and he told me there were people in the town who had heard what had been done to me and that it might cost the chief of police his job. "I think you're a skunk," the doctor said, "but even so we can't have our law men here acting like a bunch of rabid apes."

The zinc oxide felt good on the scabs.

The doctor said the idea was to put me together as good as possible in the next three weeks, in time for my arraignment in circuit court after I'd been indicted by the grand jury. He said if Circuit Judge Horace Swanburne saw my face in such a fix it would prejudice the judge against the prosecution and the judge would not admit my confession as competent evidence in the murder trial.

I sat up, "Confession, what confession?"

"Your confession to the police," the doctor said. "They say you spilled the whole works. In detail. All except the kind of car and whoever you were with. And they've sent your gun and the bullets from the bodies to FBI ballistics in Washington. You're done for, boy." He appeared pleased that I was done for.

I said, "I haven't signed anything."

He said, "You don't have to, because every officer in the department will swear from the stand you confessed, that you were not under duress, and if the judge throws out the confession he's calling them liars, or idiots, or both. Unless, of course, he denies admission of the confession on the grounds it was obtained under pressure. That's possible; but still he'd be calling them liars."

"And the ballistics?" I said. "That's competent evidence?"

"Ah, yes. The ballistics is competent. That's the thing that will burn you for sure." He smiled. "How're the fingers today?"

"Fine."

Jailer Turner Lovett came to the door, and said, "Kenneth, Nona's downstairs to see you. Nona Hickman." The doctor finished tightening the bandage on one of the splints, got his things together, and Lovett let him out of the cell. I couldn't say anything at all. Lovett waited. "You hear me, Kenneth?"

"Say it again," I said. "Say it again, slow."

"Nona wants to see you, she wants to come up here." His voice was sly and obscene. He was one of those white old men with very black hair on his hands, and I'd disliked him as a boy and I disliked him as a man.

My face puckered and all the scabs began stinging at once and I lay down on my back on the cot and looked at the ceiling. Lovett leaned back against the bars of the cell and I could hear the butt of his gun clinking against the iron as he waited. I couldn't think, or I wouldn't. Finally he left me there and I heard him going down the steel stairs and then he was back in the corridor outside the cell and she was with him. I rolled over on my side on the cot and made myself look at her and it was the hardest thing I ever had to do, much worse than the cigars and the pliers and the twisting. She took in my face without flinching, without Registering anything, and Lovett said we could talk through the bars for fifteen minutes, then he'd be up for her. The last thing he said to her was, "Miss Nona, with the town all up in the air over this, I don't think you better stay even fifteen minutes if you can cut it shorter."

And she said, "Thank you, Turner, I'll use my fifteen minutes. All of them."

She had a little rectangular package wrapped in a white starched napkin and she stooped and set it down through the bars on the floor of the cell. "Come over here, Ken. Come over here closer to me."

"I'm not coming over anywhere." I managed to sneer through the scabs. "You small-town dames give me a great big roaring pain. You fool around in a porch swing and it isn't enough that it's good and that it's what you wanted. It's got to be love." Her face went white and she hung onto the bars as if I'd hit her. I steadied my voice and went on with it. "You go drooling around the rest of your small, stinking little lives, making something pretty and spiritual out of it."

"Ken, I know what you're doing."

"You gave me what I wanted and judging from the look on your silly little go-to-church face I gave you what you wanted. But now we've got to sit here and mewl and puke around as if what I gave you was the Holy Grail. You don't undress a girl to give her the Holy Grail."

I pushed my fists down against my sides hard and when her face broke I turned away from her. But what would you have done? With the town boiling mad, did she have any business dirtying herself with a mess like this? Her steps on the stairs were fast and uneven.

That night when I got around to opening the little package I found a slab of devil's-food cake and a pack of Philip Morris cigarettes and two homemade pimiento cheese sandwiches. I took all of it over to the cot and laid it there on the gray blanket and picked up each thing and felt it a long time. I cried all over the sandwiches and when I got to where I could eat them the bread was curled and hard and the cheese was dry. O'Malley and Moore would have loved to have seen me lying there in the dark with a stale sandwich on my chest, crying my lousy heart out.

The next morning shortly after breakfast they brought Virginia in. I heard her voice downstairs and it could have been no other voice so there was no wondering about it. "Get your filthy hands off me!"

Then some shuffling down the stairwell, far below my cell, and: "Lady, if you'll please quit jumping around I'll let loose of you." Almost courtly. Apparently the report from FBI ballistics had not been received. Then the pinging scrape of feet on the steel stairs and there she was in the corridor, twenty feet away, walking straight toward me on her high red heels, swinging along with her dancer's walk, ignoring the deputy behind her. "Sweetie, what have these mongrel baboons done to you? Oh, my darling!" She ran to me, reaching through the bars for me, clawing my arms with those long nude-looking unpainted fingernails, trying to kiss me through the bars and knocking her little tan go-to-hell hat off on the floor.

"Baby, don't tear the place down." I grinned and suddenly the scabs didn't hurt; and there was the strangest thing happening to me, the old feeling of toughness and smartness drifting back into me, along with the smell of her perfume, her natural baby-smelling perfume. My scabs became more than scabs.

They took on something of dash and glamour and the splints on the broken fingers appeared rather rakish.

"You've shaved your mustache," she said. "And where are your lovely William Holdenish spectacles?"

"I don't need them any more," I said. "Everybody around here knows this is me."

"Lady, if you'll come this way," the deputy said humbly.

"Tim, it was the bullets," she said, ignoring the deputy. "It was shoot, shoot, shoot, all over the place and I never saw so damn many bullets or I wouldn't've left you, sweetie. I was sore at you, but I wouldn't have left you there alone. You know that."

"I know." And all of a sudden I honestly did, or I thought I did. She was lovely. I wanted to touch her all over and all at once and with her there before me Nona was nothing more than a piece of stale cake and some bread. Virginia was like that, she had the power to blot out other women whenever she wanted. I've seen her come into a roomful of pretty women, like Loralee and the others, women who, until Virginia came in, had pretty figures and good strong clear coloring. But when Virginia was there they lost shape and texture and tone and as long as she stayed you might as well have been looking at the others through the butt end of a Coke bottle.

"Lady," the deputy said.

"You be quiet, Grandpa, this is my boy. Oh, Tim, it's been miserable without you. I circled back into town that night. At first I drove out in the country but it was scary, and I came back and there was a hell of a crowd around the City Hall and in the concrete pit around the police station. I could hear you screaming in there."

"I was in fine voice," I said.

Another deputy came up the stairs, a bigger and less kindly one, and they took Virginia back down the corridor to a cell there on the right of the corridor, about a dozen paces from mine. My cell was at the dead end of the corridor where the stairs came up from below, and it seemed to have heavier, closer spaced bars than the others. And now I realized I'd been so busy being tough and colorful, so wrapped up in the sight of her I hadn't even asked about her arrest. Apparently they questioned her at the police station or outside somewhere because after the deputies left no one came up to see her that afternoon. And she didn't come to the door of her cell. I guess she was sleeping.

I knew that there were three cells between mine and hers. In the one nearest me there was a giant Negro with a shaven head, whose name was Harvester McCormick Tractor Jones, and he was serving time for assault and battery with intent to kill. Beyond him was a smaller Negro with a shaven head, who looked so much like the big one that he gave the impression of being a trick-mirror reflection of Harvester McCormick Tractor Jones. I don't know what his name was, only that he'd been caught operating a stumphole whisky still for a white man in the Piney woods. Jones called him Short. Not Shorty but just Short. Beyond him was a white man named Jimmie, who had made a living as a gambler until he killed another gambler who, he said, cheated him. Jimmie said this other gambler had the card game rigged in a small room with a red-diamond pattern on the wallpaper and he and his crony cut out one of the diamonds and fixed it so it would flap out on a hinge. So the crony could spy on Jimmie's hand of cards. Then the crony, sitting behind the tricky wall, would signal the crooked gambler with an electric key that made a short rod come up out the floor and tap against the sole of the crooked gambler's shoe: One tap for an ace. Two for a deuce, and so on, with special combines for the face-cards and for flushes and straights. And beyond Jimmie's cell was Virginia's.

The day after she came was Sunday and the city chaplain, a fellow who Jimmie told me later had flunked out as pastor of a regular church, came and stood in the corridor, using a music stand for a pulpit and preaching about a "bruised reed." I do not remember the significance of the bruised reed, but however it got bruised was the point of the sermon, I imagine. The Reverend Penney pronounced it *broozed*, rather than bruised. I've seen the Reverend Penney a number of Sundays since then and always meant to ask him about the reed.

When he was through preaching he asked if any-one wanted to make a testimonial. Harvey McCormick said in his deep, brooding voice that he had one to make and he made it: "I want to say that whereas I done stomped my woman and shove an ice pick in her hiney I won't do it again if there is an again for me; and that I've done seen the light and see it plain, and praise be to the Lord, Amen."

The smaller Negro said when it came his turn to testify: "I never brought nothing but desolation behind me and to both sides of me and I'm saying right now, right chere, I'm taking the Lord in with me forever and ever, Amen."

The Reverend Penney smiled and turned to Jimmie who said he had no testimonial and that furthermore he was sick of hearing the two niggers make the same ones over and over every Sunday; that if he had to listen to that sort of thing he couldn't help it, but the least he could do was not to add to the din; and that aside from this he had known Harvey McCormick all his life and as long as there were ice picks and women to shove them in, Harvey would keep right on shoving. "Why, you run religion like the cigarette companies run their business," Jimmie said reprovingly to the Reverend Penney. "I, Jimmie, find religion is good. None of the harsh irritants of sin in it. Testimonials! My God!"

The Reverend Penney smiled and opened his hymn book and picked out a number and laid the book on the music stand.

Then he walked along the corridor, handing each

of us a book, except Jimmie, who wouldn't reach for it. I saw Virginia's hand come out and take one and later, when the singing started, I was surprised she knew the tune to "Holy, Holy, Holy." Her voice was true and high against the voices of the Negroes, and what she was singing wasn't "Holy, Holy, Holy" at all, but the preacher and the others were too involved in their own racket to notice.

What she sang, fitting the words into the cadence of the spiritual, was that the police had the Packard and her gun and all the clothes and money in it (we'd banked all but about $3,000, spreading it thin over a number of banks so as not to arouse suspicion) and that they had found the car where she abandoned it in the woods, later the night after my arrest, after she'd come into town and driven out again; and that they caught her in a cab on the edge of town headed for New Orleans, when the cab driver told his dispatcher to radio police that a woman had offered him two hundred dollars for a thirty-five-dollar ride to New Orleans; that she'd spent most of the time prior to her own arrest in a small hotel in Masonville, dead drunk, afraid to wiggle one way or the, other, since the town was stirred up and since she knew the kind of treatment I'd received. The hymn had four stanzas. Then we began "Love Lifted Me," a much slower one, very poor for Virginia's purposes, and all she was able to get across to me during this one was that we had to agree on some kind of story, a common story, hanging the murder of the policemen (the *opps-kay*) on someone else. Some strangers in a green car. The Reverend Penney and the Negroes sang in three entirely different keys and Penney swung wide of the tune on the corners and I had to listen sharp to get any of what she sang to me. The word "murder" sounds odd in a hymn. So does the word "gun." It's no wonder you never find either of them printed into the hymns.

That night the Reverend Penney returned to his iron-bound flock and there was more preaching and singing.

And this time I got the hang of it and was able to get through to Virginia via the hymns. But clumsily, not nearly so well as she did it. I saw Jimmie looking at me peculiarly once and I began singing the real words to the song until he left the door of his cell.

The Reverend Penney threw his arms around when he sang and rocked back and forth and it was so strenuous and demanding the way he did it I don't guess he had time to listen to all the questions and answers Virginia and I were singing to each other. You could tell he was a devoted man. Indeed a dedicated man. But at the same time he was so awed and occupied with himself and what God did for, and meant, to him, that there was something disinterested in his dealings with his flock. A man has only so much energy and so much power of concentration. Harvey McCormick Tractor Jones and the smaller Negro, after the fashion of their race, were more concerned with the melody than the words, and the way it came out of those dark throats was a wonderful thing to hear. No one could sing that beautifully and at the same time listen to anyone else.

Jimmie was the only one who worried me. But I believed his bitterness toward the law would seal him tight, even if he heard.

By the time the grand jury went into session Virginia and I, through the medium of hymns, had worked out a logical and fairly melodious story for the trial. It was built around a nonexistent green car, and if it flopped it was still better than no story at all.

There were about three or four days between the time the grand jury convened and the time we actually were arraigned on the murder charges, and I slept poorly at night during this period. I could lie on my cot and see down the hall to Virginia's cell, the barred door of it narrowed by the slanting angle. I had only a small slit in a window in my cell but there must have been a larger window in hers because some nights the moonlight would come gushing broadly out of her cell, almost bright as day against the floor of the corridor down there. I'd roll over on my stomach, looking at the moonlight and knowing it had washed over her between window and corridor, and wondering how she looked with all that cream-colored hair curving against her pillow in the silver-blue light. I ached for the feel of her, for the smooth miracle of her beautiful body, for the color of her eyes near mine. Nona? Who was Nona?

I wanted Virginia, She was a creature of moonlight, crazy as moonlight, all upthrusting radiance and hard silver dimples and hollows, built for one thing and only one thing and perfectly for that. I chewed my knuckles and wanted Virginia. I watched the moonlight spill down through the bars of the door of her cell and wondered how I'd ever thought I was sick of a thing as good as Virginia.

Then I was sitting on my cot, arms stiff against the mattress, blinking.

Turner Lovett, the jailer, was down there outside her door, looking around. Apparently he couldn't see me in the darkness at the dead end of the corridor, but he looked down my way a long time before he fitted the key into her door. Metal scratched lightly against metal and he removed the key, pulled the door open and slid inside, closing it behind him and locking it from within. I saw his fist clamped onto one of the vertical bars as he pulled the door inward until it fitted the sill, then the scratching again, of the key. The moonlight gilded the heavy hairs on his fingers. For the next hour I sat there, sweating, gripped in a pure agony of hate and desire and something else I couldn't begin to explain to you. Whatever it was it shriveled me and weakened me and in the morning I wanted nothing to eat.

The following night I waited for Lovett, never taking my eyes off the corridor for more than a few seconds, watching it even as I lit cigarettes, staring down there at the door of her cell. The walls kept pushing in on me, closer and closer, and I remember that I wanted to jump up on the cot and swing out my arms and push them away from me so I could breathe and think this thing out to its black, filthy limit. It was bad enough in New Orleans, her skating around with Eddie and coming back to me with that exaggeratedly matter-of-fact look in the lavender-gray eyes, saying: "Did you miss me? Were we gone long, sweetie?" You could blame that on the money and the quaint, historic, fornicating atmosphere of old New Orleans, the wealthy unfettered atmosphere, something nice after a lean spell for a money-drunk girl, who'd been hounded out of a fat spot in New York. You could blame that on all sorts of things. But this was the jailer. To be there in that stinking cell on a dirty cot with a poor, bald-headed, hairy-handed goat, you couldn't chalk that off to atmosphere.

At about one in the morning Lovett popped into the moonlight outside her door and went inside as before.

I heard her giggle, the cot creaked twice, loudly, and there was silence. I heard her say, "No, wait a minute, Turner." The cot creaked again, louder. And there was a dull thump and then a lot of thumps and a low groan.

The door of the cell swung open and here she came down the hall, swinging her hips and holding the keys high and to the side in the moonlight where I could see them. Halfway to me she pivoted, returned to her cell, and locked the door behind her. When finally she let me out we almost ate each other up. Then: "Tim, the old fool won't stay out forever. We better go on down and get out of here before he yells." She said he had told her there was no one downstairs in the jailer's quarters except Mrs. Lovett and her daughter and that you couldn't wake them with a bugle once they began sleeping and snoring. He was right about the snoring. At the foot of the stairs you could hear it. There was a barred iron gate there separating the stairwell from the reception room, or whatever you want to call it. I got in too big a hurry and spent five minutes trying to find the proper key on the ring. Each key looked huger than the one before it, much too big for the keyhole. And all the keys rattled and clinked and whanged like chimes against one another and against the ring and the door. "Hurry, Tim, I think I heard something upstairs." And the more I hurried the worse it was, until I got the right key into the hole. "Tim, there really is something moving around up there. It must be Lovett," We were across the reception room and working at the lock of the outer door and Virginia's breathing was faster and faster, but no faster than my own. "Hurry, for God's sake, hurry," she said.

Outside, walking toward the New Orleans highway, she said, "I hit him with a stool, a very small stool. It won't last long. But my God, it was fine to hit him." She laughed and squeezed my hand. We didn't see anyone in the streets except a man in coveralls going somewhere to work, coughing and hawking, trying to get rid of last night's cigarettes. I knew all the side streets. There was the feeling of going somewhere, going somewhere new, and then the big diesel trucks were whooshing by on the highway and we were standing in the tall wet grass flagging a ride to New Orleans. Virginia was nervous and doubtful. "It's just a matter of percentage," I told her. "Out of every ten or twenty trucks there is one driver who is neither chicken nor afraid."

The one driver who was neither chicken nor afraid was about my size and age. Virginia sat between us and whenever he shifted gears he managed to brush the back of his hand against her leg.

Virginia whispered to me, "You know, if I'd thought we weren't going to get to use our story about the green car, I'd've not sung all those howling hymns. I wish there were some way now to un-sing them. Especially "Love Lifted Me.""

The driver looked around at us. He was not a bad fellow, but he did not like a girl to whisper to another man so soon after he touched her leg. It must have been disconcerting. I didn't blame him for glaring, because he had done it with a nice skill, so that it looked more like shifting gears than petting, but with plenty of petting in it, a niceness of balance and application worthy of a nobler enterprise. To Virginia, this casual touch probably meant no more than putting on her shoes, and that is one fine thing about a woman that you do not find in a lady. A woman does not blow up the importance of a minor thing like swapping a feel of the leg for a ride, intimacy being a relative element and one which a woman understands in its true light. The tires hummed steadily on the moist concrete and Virginia told the trucker he was a fine driver and after that he didn't glare, but talked of his wife and some kind of operation she had as the result of falling on a bicycle seat. The trucker said she fell on the seat years ago, but that the doctor told her it was in a place she wouldn't notice for a long time and only then if it were repeatedly irritated. "Female trouble," the trucker said, getting the authentic tone into it. "There's all kinds of female trouble. My sister lost all her organs last year. One at a time. Every month they found something new to take out of her."

"That's the way it is," Virginia said, putting sympathy into it.

"Yeah, dames're funny machines. With a truck you just go in there and tear out the whole rear end and be done with it," the trucker said.

When he let us out we knew all about his wife and sister, and we were good friends.

We knew that by morning the New Orleans papers would be smeared with us, black with us. We couldn't go to any New Orleans bank after our names, and my alias, became public property, so the best thing to do was get out of there, and the faster the better. I told

Virginia if only we had the money to fly to Denver and then go on up to Cripple Creek in the mountains where nobody thought to look for anybody, that we could camp up there until the heat cooled.

"I've got the money," she said.

She said the night we were separated after the shooting she got to mulling over the way I'd once had her sew some bills in the panel of a girdle. "I had a girdle and I had some money, so I did it. Does it show?"

"No, how much?"

"Three thousand."

"Dollars?"

"What do you think, pianos?"

"Glory be, baby."

"Glory be to the both of us—for our own glory."

So we flew to Denver, paid four hundred for a jeep, and headed back for the rocks as fast as our little wheels would carry us.

~§~

The very tip of the hollow cooking rock stuck darkly out of the snow and there was snow in the hollow of it, mounded high and round like an ice cream cone. The baby cliff which had served as a sleeping shelter last summer was topped with a frozen ledge of whiteness and our swimming pool was a blue glut of ice. We'd left the jeep on the road and climbed the slope together to the campsite, wearing the ski suits and boots we bought in Colorado Springs. Virginia was something to see in a ski suit and a Norwegian sweater with reindeer prancing on the front and all around it. Her bosom bent the reindeer out of shape. She'd lost her hotel fat and the old money-sickness too, I believe, and now it seemed she enjoyed floundering around in the snow up there and using her feet to walk on. I scooped the snow out of the basin of the cooking rock and lifted her up and sat her in the hollow, and I remember we sang and laughed like a couple of loons. My face was almost completely healed and when she rubbed snow into it, we felt good, stingingly good. And we were free. For a while at any rate. We drank from a pint of Harper and chased it with mouthfuls of snow and the whisky went down hot and round as a poker, burning bright in the stomach, then sifting warmly down through the legs and feet, sending little showers of warmness down there. Then we were serious for a time and I leaned against the rock and put my arms around her and kissed her and held her closer and tighter; and the kissing was better and better in the stinging air, until finally I slid her off the rock into the snow. The snow was soft and there was no coldness to it.

It was snowing when we went back to the jeep, the flat khaki-painted hood of the secondhand car white with it and the canvas top sagging under the curve of white.

We finished the bottle in the jeep and I pulled out

some gum and we each chewed a piece and it was so cold it broke like glass in our mouths. Until it warmed, the pieces wouldn't stick together in a wad.

Then abruptly I wondered if the custodian of armored car twelve ever had that trouble in cold weather, since he was a man fond enough of gum to smuggle a carton or so into the hereafter with him; and if the water in the shaft was frozen now; and I wondered if he were frozen in a solid block of clear ice in the car, his face against the slits, peering through the ice beyond the car. And at what? We hadn't visited the shaft and now I shook it out of my head and we drove on down to the Imperial Hotel. Killing the two cops had never punished me like killing the custodian. When a man points a gun at you or shoots at you, you feel differently than if he simply drops an empty gum package on your foot. You notice I said killing the two cops? I'd got so in the habit of taking all the blame when the police were pushing the cigars into me that now the pattern was sort of burned into me. I seldom thought of Virginia as having killed the blond one and launching the whole mess.

We spent the night in the hotel and the manager told us that if we had trouble getting water out of the faucets to call him. "Now and then I find a rainbow trout in the meter," he said. "And sometimes other fish, smaller ones. It's easy to fix."

The manager was a young man with a bashful manner and we learned later he had been a ski trooper in Italy during the war. His wife was young, too, and they borrowed all the money they could lay their hands on to raise a down payment on the hotel and were buying it mostly on guts and imagination, bringing in the melodrama troupe each summer as an added drawing card and running a modest ski school in the winters. Virginia and I were just people to Wayne and Dorothy Mackin and they were much too busy running the hotel to ask us any detailed questions about ourselves.

The days fell into a relaxing pattern of skiing, or rather learning to ski, eating heavy spiced meals of meat and potatoes, sprawling around the lobby in the evenings with the other skiers, drinking a blackish drink that was mostly rum, and which for some reason skiers fancy above others in that part of the world. The skiing crowd came on weekends and there were no regulars in the middle of the week that winter, except us. We were on the second floor near the staircase and most of the time the fifty other rooms were vacant.

It was fine, but when you are afraid and running from something, the better time you have the worse the suspense you'll be caught. Or so I've found it. When you're having a splendid time the suspense is doubled and redoubled until the fine time collapses around your ears, if you aren't careful.

Our faces and necks and hands were burned a deep chocolate red by the winter sun and at night after we came up to the room from the lobby we were pleasantly tired. Despite the sparkling near-zero cold we slept with the big windows open some nights, piling the feathered comforters high and propping up on our pillows to gaze out at the cold stars and talk of the strangeness and satisfaction of our life together. Virginia never mentioned New Orleans any more, nor New York and Beekman Place. We had read, in a Colorado Springs paper, an Associated Press story that stated what we already knew, that she, too, was wanted for murder.

The ballistics report checked solid against the pearl-handled automatic found in the car, and her fingerprints, taken the day of her arrest, were all over the car and the gun. Kenneth Hawkins had issued an elaborate statement about all this. I told Virginia I'd never heard of a woman going to the chair for murder, or anything else, in Mississippi. She said there had to be a first time for everything and with the kind of luck she'd had all her life it would be just like her to start a new legal fad down there if they caught us. She had her pillow doubled and wadded behind her shoulders and the back of her head against the solid headboard of the old-fashioned bed. "Tim, I've always felt I'd die young, and horribly."

The way she said that sent the shivers up me. "Is the electric chair really horrible?"

"I don't know."

"Does smoke come out of them when they turn the juice on, Tim, like they say in the paper?"

"For God's sake, Virginia."

"No, darling, I'm not joking, I mean it."

"Well, forget it."

"I read once that this man was in the chair and when the electrocutioner threw the switch the smoke came out of the man's head and formed a question mark over him and everybody said it was an omen, that maybe he didn't commit the murder they killed him for."

"Well," I said, "if they catch me, there won't be any question mark. There'll be an exclamation point."

"Do you really think so?" she said in a perfectly serious voice.

"Of course not. Now for Pete's sake shut up, baby, about all that burning." I pulled the covers around my neck. "We're not burning, we're freezing."

"Tim, do they really shave your head?"

"Yes."

"To let the electricity get in it?"

"I guess so."

"I should hate that, sweetie."

She moved close to me, bumping sideways in the bed, like a child, and yet not at all like a child. "And they have a roomful of people watching you when they throw the switch, that's what I hate most, watching the way they would a tennis match, and seeing you later when you're all ugly."

"Baby, just about anywhere you die there's somebody watching. It doesn't make any difference whether they're watching you die in bed or in a chair, somebody's going to be there. It's strictly a spectator sport."

She rolled over and slid her arm across my chest.

"That's a nice way to look at it."

"It's the only way to look at it."

She shivered, holding me tightly to her. The winter stars blinked distantly in the wind and they were never dearer to me. The light crested the ragged snowline of the mountains beyond the window, pure and clear, dancing against the ridges. "Does it ever bother you a lot, darling, that I am what I am?"

"No." I kissed her on the nose and it was cold and innocent as a button.

"Honestly, Tim?"

"No, the only time you bother me is when you're not what you are."

"That's a lovely thing to say."

"I'm not trying to be lovely. I'm telling you what I think."

"Anyway it's lovely." She was biting my cheek, my right cheek, the one Moore and O'Malley had liked. "Tim, did you ever think that the very fact I'm bad is really a kind of tribute to you, since I've known them all sizes and all ages and all temperatures and *know* what I want in a man?"

"I've thought of it."

"And if you're willing to discount the nastiness, doesn't it make you feel a little conceited?"

"A very little."

"You're lying, darling."

"A little."

"Whenever I used to see married men jerking their lawful wedded wives in and out of cars and steering them down the sidewalks like wheelbarrows it tickled me," she said. "There's something so comical about that kind of possessiveness. Because you can't own anybody by shielding them and bullying them and spying on them. It's just the other way 'round."

"That's not exactly a new idea."

"It's not a popular one either. It's like the electric chair. No matter what I start thinking I wind up with the chair, don't I? Because I know I'm going to die horribly as anyone can die."

And she was right.

But that night I didn't believe her . . .

~§~

Around the middle of December we rented a small two-bed-room cottage south of the hotel. It cost only fifteen dollars a month. Cripple Creek is not quite a ghost town and not quite a live one either. It is deserted except for a few families and most of the men are either miners or commute to Colorado Springs. It is a real estate agent's nightmare, in that you can buy a four-bedroom house for little more than a thousand dollars, yet in most cases untangling titles is next to impossible for records have long since been lost or were burned in the great fire that almost flattened the town years past.

Virginia talked more and more frequently of dying, and I don't know if she truly felt that way or if it was her way of cracking the monotony, but on Christmas Eve she kicked over the Christmas tree and staged a long, violent crying jag. She said the Christmas tree lights used the same kind of electricity that was used in the electric chair and she would be damned if she'd have it in the house. Then she took off her shoe and began dragging a chair around the house and batting out the regular overhead lights until I stopped her. She fought me like a wild woman until she passed out.

Part VI

Chapter Thirteen

I TOOK TO GOING out by myself on the skis, climbing the tall slopes west of the town and messing around and practicing by myself until I became fairly skillful. But there was a funny thing. It seemed the shaft of the old Katie Lewellyn was always in the back of my head and every day it kept pulling me closer and closer to it when I made these trips up there. I could feel the pull of it. And whenever I came in sight of the tall crooked outbuilding near the shaft I'd stop and lean on my poles and stare at it until the sweat began popping out beneath the windproof clothes. The old building was partly broken in the middle and with the torn batwing of shingles on top like a fingernail, it looked like a giant finger of wood, crooked at me, beckoning. And the custodian had long since crowded Jeepie from my dreams, coming into them in many forms, but always in water and ice. Sometimes he was damp, and again he was drenched or blowing nightmare bubbles through the slits of the armored car and whining, always whining or moaning of the cold. Sometimes he regarded me from a clear bell of ice, and once from a little temple of ice the shape of those things you see along the road in the pictures of Burma. And he was black and rigid with cold.

I kept telling myself it was silly to think a dead man in the bottom of a six-hundred-foot hole could keep pulling me and pulling me back to the area of the shaft. I told myself it was the lure of the gold, the knowledge that once men had torn it from the earth there. I told myself I was getting gold-happy like everyone else in Cripple Creek, and they are that, because even the town doctor and the mayor go out in the hills in their spare time and whack away at the rocks with miners' picks. I'd borrowed some books from the Mackins, telling about the evolution of gold mining, and how long ago a cowboy named Bob Womack stumbled onto a fortune in the yellow metal and got drunk and gambled away his claim. And I'd read a book put out by the Denver mint, this one also borrowed from the Mackins and also dealing with precious metals. It said more than $158,000,000 worth of gold ingots can be stacked in a cage five feet square and ten feet high. The pamphlet said a million dollars worth of platinum can be tidily hidden beneath an army cot. It said also that the men who work in the mint at Denver punching out silver dollars and fifty-cent pieces make no more than eight or ten dollars a day, yet one man in eight hours can punch out more than a half-million silver dollars, enough to pay him and all his buddies their salaries for the rest of their lives. I read, too, about vanadium and copper and zinc and alumi-num. But it wasn't the idea of metal that kept sucking me in ever tightening circles to the old Katie Lewellyn.

I wanted to look down that hole.

I had the absolutely senseless feeling that perhaps if I looked into the shaft I'd see something down there in the blackness. That maybe this something would ease my mind, or maybe it would drive me stark raving mad, but whatever, I wanted to look. Like a kid who in the middle of the night thinks there's something under his bed.

Chapter Fourteen

ONE AFTERNOON IN THE middle of January, an afternoon when Virginia was feeling gayer than usual, we decided to make up some sandwiches and spend the rest of the day on skis and eat somewhere in the hills above town. She had her good days along with the bad, stretches when she was the same tough, beautiful Virginia of last year. There were these brief periods when she said nothing and apparently thought nothing of the dying business. During these times it was as if she couldn't get enough of sensory pleasure, of loving, of eating and drinking, of smells and colors.

We climbed to the crest of Eagle Ridge and ate the sandwiches there and washed them down with hot cocoa from a thermos, then kicked off the skis and walked around up there in the sunshine.

There was a six foot cradle of granite and I slapped the snow out of it with my mittens and we sat there and smoked, still warmed by the cocoa and the food, and enjoying the view from the ridge, hating to leave it. You could see for miles in all directions and I pointed out the building near the Katie Lewellyn and the piles of tailings near several other shafts and we talked about whether or not Golden Cycle was making a lot of money by reworking the Molly Kathleen and how the new machinery was able to process lower-grade ores at a profit. But Virginia kept turning the talk back to the Katie Lewellyn and it was as if she shared the strange feeling about it that I did. She said the Mackins told her that in some of the water-filled shafts like the Katie they had installed pumps so they could get back into them with the new machinery and work them, and that in one they had drilled through from another shaft at a lower level and were letting the water drain out that way.

I reminded her of what the bartender told us the first time we were in the Gold Bar, of how he had said the Katie Lewellyn was never much of a mine at its best; and that there wasn't much chance our secret would ever be uncovered in this world.

"He wouldn't know," Virginia said. "He was just some college boy earning a summer vacation in the mountains."

I didn't say anything. I was thinking of how it would feel to be the member of a pumping crew sent down into the Katie Lewellyn for preliminary survey after the water had been knocked out of her. How did they make their first trip down? On ladders? Or did they set up the cage and lower it from a cable spool, and what kind of light would they have when they reached the bottom and saw the armored car glinting in the shaft, its round rivet-heads glowing, the slits in its walls black and silent? I felt certain that in the fall the heavy iron car had torn free of the shell of the house trailer, and that that was what we heard, that metallic screaming, after we dropped the trailer in the shaft that night in September.

The sun was behind a thready gray cloud now and the wind stiffened on the ridge.

"Tim, we'd better be moving."

"Yes." I helped her into the mess of straps and buckles of the skis, noting for the thousandth time how short and wide and babylike her feet looked. Even more so, in the box-toed ski boots, Then I got into my own harness and we started down the curving gentle slope, and below the level of the ridge it was not so cold.

Down the trail the slope flattened into a kind of plateau and we moved along side by side for a good eight hundred yards to the edge of this where the slope was renewed and from here we had a detailed view of the Katie Lewellyn, which lay between us and the town. The trail swung wide to the left of the shaft, but as we left the plateau I moved off the trail and angled south and Virginia followed without saying anything. Now we could see the jeep where we'd left it on the main road where we began the climb; and it was as if long ago we'd agreed that we would do this thing, and now with the skis slicing cleanly down the slope toward the mine I felt a peculiar sense of relief, as if some weight had been lifted from me. Virginia was right on my heels all the way down. The noon sun had melted the snow slightly and now it was hardening into a crust of frozen clots which glittered roundly. It was perfect for skiing and I don't believe either of us had ever done so well. It is the nearest thing there is to flying. And once your legs and ankles are in shape for it, it is almost effortless as the flight of a bird unless you are doing something fancy or reckless.

Near the mine it flattened out again into another midget plateau and you had to mush it slow and clumsy near the hole and there is no more ridiculous feeling than slopping along this way on the big waxed slats after you have been flying. We sat down on a clutter of ancient timbers, a dozen yards from the shaft, after I'd leaned the skis against the outbuilding. The blood was lumping and pumping and lumping and pumping in my throat and when I tried to smoke the cigarette tasted like tin.

I knew I had to look in that hole.

I put my arm around Virginia. She hadn't said a word since we left Eagle Ridge. I put my hand under her chin and pulled her face around and kissed her.

"Tim, I hate you to do that when you aren't thinking what you're doing." She leaned away from me. She sat there on the timbers, her long slim legs spraddled out stiff, the weight of them against the heels in the snow. She chopped absently at the snow with a ski pole. Finally she said with a shiver, "It's as if all the evil we know is down there in the pit."

I tried to laugh. "Oh, not all of it, baby. Not in one little old six-hundred-foot hole. You underestimate us."

I tried another cigarette and this one tasted better and I gave her one, lit it for her. "Virginia, I'm going to have to look at the shaft."

"Sure," she kept chopping at the snow between her heels with the pole. "I knew you would."

"And you?"

"Yes, Tim, I have to look, too. God knows why, but I have to look."

All the color had left her face. Her voice was sick and thin. I patted her mitten. "Baby, you feel all right?" She raised her eyes slowly from the lip of the shaft and looked at me, her face unmoving, the gaze steady.

"I've the feeling, Tim, this thing, this thing we're doing now, is going to kill us or cure us." She put her hand against my mouth. "No, don't joke, for God's sake don't joke now." She glanced at the shaft as if it might be listening, keeping the mitten against my mouth so that I could feel the trembling inside the dark scratchy wool.

I asked her again if she felt all right.

"I feel like a ghoul. I feel all right for a ghoul."

"Baby, we don't really have to look in that hole," I

said, knowing I lied, knowing that the hideous magnet in the cold guts of the Katie Lewellyn dragged harder at me this instant than ever before. A slow sickening whirl seemed to move around and past us, as if the air itself had become so thick with evil as to be a tangible force, emptying into the pit, tugging at us, wanting to take us with it. It was the kind of sickness I once felt as a boy, running to show my mother a baby robin I'd found in the Crepe Myrtle, and before I reached her I fell, my weight on the hand with the bird. It was a blind disgust so intense, so very much of what it was, as to carry with it a terrible fascination. The ultimate in horror is, for some unworldly reason, attractive. Hypnotic. For this reason you stare at the face of a leper at Carville. You are riveted at the scene of an automobile smash-up. You may loathe high places and leap irresistibly into the very space that fills you with nausea. A man terrified of snakes may spend hours watching the green metallic head of the python in the cage.

"Tim?" She was holding my hand.

"What, baby?"

"I'm all right now."

I got up and started toward the hole, taking small slow steps in the snow and watching ahead of me, and the blood kept piling up in my throat until I thought I would strangle. My knees were having a time with the weight of my body. They didn't shake exactly, but they weren't right.

"Wait a minute, Tim. I'm coming with you, ok? I'm

damned if I'll look into it later, alone."

I heard the small square feet crunching against the snow and then her hand was on my arm and we were moving toward the lip of the shaft together, the wind in cold gusts at our backs, and I wanted to lie down and crawl the last six feet. And I did. And so did Virginia. Both of us on our bellies, her elbow bumping against mine as we edged toward it. There was a broken pick handle frozen tight and slantingly in the earth, maybe two feet from the rim of the hole, and when we reached this Virginia nudged me to move left so she could come around it on the same side with me. She didn't want even the pick handle between us, and now I could hear her crying, really bawling, unashamedly, and it was very loud there in the stillness on the edge of the wickedness that was the Katie Lewellyn. She broke it off in a shuddering sigh when I dropped flat on my belly and pulled her down against me, but she kept whim-pering for maybe fifteen minutes and we just lay there, still a foot short of being able to look down over the edge of the thing. "Tim, she said brokenly, "I can't stand it." I told her to turn around and crawl back to the skis and I would be with her in a minute. "No," she said, "I couldn't stand not to look either. I think I'm going crazy. I've got to look at it and I can't, like a woman who's known for months she had a cancer and the doctor finally tells her it's there and he tells her where to look to see it. And she must look at it but she can't."

"I know, Virginia."

"Do you, do you really know, about the cancer part of it, what I mean about the cancer?"

"It's eating me, too, baby." Her body jerked almost convulsively against me and her breath on my face was hot and dry. Her eyes, the lovely lavender-gray eyes of Virginia, were very wide and oddly glazed and the brown speckles in them floated big on the surface, each speckle with shape and texture of its own. "Oh, my God," she said, her voice wound-up tight. "Oh, my good heavenly God help me."

"You go on back to the skis." I rolled away from her, firming my voice, patting her back and smiling at her. The smile must have been a dry, comic thing to see, because my mouth was so cottony that my lips wouldn't slide right. With my lip stuck up high on my teeth I must have looked like a panic-stricken Eskimo dog.

"I'm not going back," she said. "Doctor, I'm ready, show me the goddamned cancer."

Then we were propped on our elbows at the edge of the hole and I found I couldn't look down all at once into the blackness. I was going to have to look first at the top of the opposite wall and let my eyes move down it, a little at a time, getting used to it, the way you do when you're bathing in cold water—building up an immuneity to cowardice by suffering on a small scale and increasing the dose.

I could hear Virginia breathing beside me and our

breaths floated white and fluffy over the edge of the pit.

The opposite wall was plain tan dirt for maybe three or four feet down and then it blended into a rusty band of rotten rock no more than twenty inches thick. There were bits of yellowed wire sticking out of it and what seemed to be part of an ancient horse-shoe, and what it was doing there I don't know. Below the rusty band was a clearer red, speckled and streaked, and it went down and down in the fading light. All of the rock was rolled vertically, the way the curtain is draped from the overhead rod on the stage of a theatre, in long parallel wrinkles.

Away down was the sable chilliness I had dreaded, jet black and suckingly horrible.

"Geez," Virginia said.

"It's ugly, isn't it, baby?"

"If you fell in there," her teeth chattered, "you'd be insane before you ever hit bottom."

I inched back, imperceptibly, from the edge, saying, "Probably."

"But we aren't going to fall in there," she said, making a kind of question of it.

"No."

"We are going to get up and walk off from here and act as if we hadn't seen the cancer at all, but seeing it helped, didn't it? You can't fight it until you've seen it."

"A deep subject, baby."

This hit her as funny, I guess, lying on the edge of a

six-hundred-foot hole and talking about deep subjects. Anyway she laughed. And suddenly her tension appeared broken by the laughter and she was her old self again, cocky and beautiful and totally in command of herself. "Good old Doc Sunblade and his Rocky Mountain Horror Clinic," she said. Then, in a completely serious tone: "Tim, I think I'm cured; I think I'm well, rid of it."

"Fine."

"It's as if looking down there into it released me."

I knew what she meant. I began pushing back, crawfishing from the hole, my rear humped up and elbows thrusting me back and away. "Come on," I said. Virginia giggled. She got up on all fours and moved back and we climbed to our feet. She was pure radiance then, all aglow, and the very air around her seemed to crackle with confidence and she began talking about a dozen things at once, about what she was going to fix for supper and how she was going to fix it, how she wasn't going to mope around the house any more and let me go off in the hills by myself, how the Mackins said we could buy the old four-story brick railroad station if we wanted a good solid place of our own (the price was a thousand dollars), how next summer we'd move back to the campsite above Cripple Creek and swim in the old pool and sleep under the moon and live to be a thousand or more. The transformation was something to see. From a sick scared little dull-eyed blonde to the same electric Virginia who once tried to claw me to ribbons on the road outside Colorado Springs. From a whimpering, whining thing afraid of her own Christmas tree lights to a woman who spoke of the future with authority, who said "next summer" and "next winter" and "next week." I liked that. If there is anything that I miss now it is not being able to think of next summer and next winter, or even next week.

To my delight she broke into an exuberant little clog dance, so free and light and easy, so wonderfully graceful and healthy it made my chest hurt. She kicked front and back and sideways and the snow from her feet stung my face and we both began laughing and laughing and the world was a lovely white oyster and it was ours to open at that, moment. I remember thinking that Virginia in movies would have been a thing of light and a joy forever. And I hooked my arm in hers and we spun 'round and 'round in the snow, giggling like fools, braying our happiness to the heights of the frozen white hills, giddy in our reprieve. For looking into the hole had somehow been just that. A reprieve—if not a pardon.

I think if God were to say to me: "Kenneth, I'm going to let you take your pick and live again any incident in your life that gave you a particular bang," I'd pick that one on the edge of the hole when, after forcing ourselves to look into it, we felt as if we'd rid ourselves of some loathsome disease.

I remember the only thing that worried me then was that Virginia was awfully close to the hole, but she was smiling and her movements were very sure. Then all of a sudden she did a crazy little sideways jig, the way chorines do when they're leaving the stage in line, and her boot caught on the frozen pick handle and she turned slowly, very slowly and lazily, and her back arched prettily as she went over the edge into the hole.

I couldn't move. Lightning couldn't have moved me in that first instant she went down. We were having a hell of a time and then I was there all by myself, just a fellow in the snow by himself. And it seems, thinking back to it, I stood there an hour before I heard her screams from inside the hole. Before I began crawling back to it, and then I was there and the noise of the screaming was somewhere beneath me but I couldn't see her. And over all of it was the ugly smell of the damp stone and water from the shaft, as strong as the noise and the dizzying pull of the blackness. I remember scrambling around to the other side of the shaft so that I could see the wall along which she had fallen and the first thing I saw then was the cream-colored hair against the red rock of the wall.

She was face down on a narrow bow of rock, not a ledge, but a ragged slanting bulge, no more than forty feet from the surface. The bulge that broke her fall was neither as wide nor as long as her body, but an odd pommel of rock pushed up between the backs of her knees, allowing at least temporary anchorage. Her head hung down over one end of the bow of rock and her feet extended over the pit, too.

And she screamed as if she were looking down into the very pits of hell. Kept screaming.

Somehow I managed to get back to the outbuilding where our skis and the poles were leaning against the wall, and the skis were the longest so I grabbed one of them and started back. I had no idea of distances then and it seemed perfectly logical to get the ski. I recall falling and smashing my face against the heelplate of the ski and getting up and running. I remember throwing myself down on the edge of the pit and dangling the ski down there and waving it at her as if the waving would somehow lift her off the rock and bring her up to me.

Finally it dawned on me that the ski was not forty feet long and would never be forty feet long.

But I still had no more idea of the stretch of that distance than of the number of miles to the moon. I got up and sprinted back to the outbuilding and began tearing at one of the long gray boards that lined its sides, trying to tear it loose from the frame, and it wouldn't come off. My fingers were red with blood, a raw and shining red, and I knew they were hurting even though I couldn't exactly feel them, and the board would not come loose. The edges of it were slippery and wet and I remember you could see the grain of the wood plainly through the red. I went to the clutter of timbers where we'd sat and smoked when we first came down off the ridge and I found among the timbers a very long two-by-four, so long that it seemed to stretch from the pile off into the mountains, and when I'd jerked it free of the pile I held it before me like a pole-vaulter and ran with it toward the shaft. I ran as fast as I could and the timber, which seemed to scrape the sky, was without weight in my hands.

It did not reach halfway to her. And if it had, I don't know what I'd have expected her to do, down there with her poor broken body in the cold eddying edge of the blackness. I dropped it in the hole and she began screaming all over again, as if the dim sound of its plummeting in the depths below her renewed the horror for her.

"Virginia," I yelled. It went down into the hole and came back twice life-size: VIRGINIA.

She didn't answer me but the screaming dimmed into something between a whimper and a gurgle. "Virginia," I said, "I'm going into town and get some ropes and things." And the blackness of the hole bellowed back at me: AND THINGS! I had a crazy impulse to begin laughing, laughing at the top of my lungs.

It began snowing. I got onto the skis and moved down the slope to the jeep. And I remember coming into the lobby of the hotel, but nothing between the jeep and the hotel, and starting up the stairs to my room. Wayne Mackin was there and he told me hello and asked where I was going and I said I was going up to the room for a while and that I would get a rope up there if I could find one. He looked puzzled. He told me I didn't live there in the room any more and that I lived down the street in the cottage with the yellow door. I asked him who was in my room in the hotel and he said a fellow by name of Clell Dooley, which at the time meant nothing to me, nothing at all. The cottage was cold and the wind was slamming the shutters as I packed some bread and meat in a sheet of oiled paper. Rope, I thought. I need a rope. Clell Dooley, I thought. What a nice round name, round as a rope. A good name. But still there was the rope, and I looked all over the cottage without finding even a clothesline and then I took the bread and meat out to the jeep on the side of the house. Dooley. Clell Dooley. The snow was a stinging slant of white, heavy and almost opaque in the headlights. I giggled when I hit a bank of snow on the side of the road, the jeep bouncing out of it in a crazy yellow spray as the lights shone into the flurry. I drove back to the hotel, flying blind. Maybe Wayne could tell me about the rope. The lobby was empty except for a man, his back turned to me, sitting on a divan, the rear of which was made of a wagon wheel. Above the gilded curve of the rim of the wheel I saw his gray flannel shoulders and the back of his black curly head plainly and it was the head of Clell Dooley, my good FBI friend who long ago had packed me off to Parchman with a lecture on borrowing other people's automobiles. He is the only man I ever saw who could strut while he was sitting still, and there was no mistaking him. The outside cold must have cleared my fear-riddled head because now for the first time I connected the name of the man who had our old room with the Clell Dooley I knew. I turned slowly, keeping my eyes on him, and he shifted impatiently on the divan, threw down a magazine with a slap, and yawned. It was an official FBI yawn, somewhat like the yawn of Leo the Lion in the movies. He began twisting around toward me as if he felt me in the room and I moved faster then toward the door and he jumped up and stared at me as I cleared the door and hit the seat of the jeep in one flying lunge.

After that things happened fast, fast and white, because the blizzard had really declared itself by now. The jeep was thumping and bumping away from the hotel and somewhere behind me two tiny yellow lights no bigger than peas were on my trail. They got larger and brighter and then they were gone as I took a left turn, and they came back in a moment, very small, but unshrinking now. *Virginia, wait for me. Wait for me, baby.* It was snowing on Virginia. The cream hair was cold and salted with snow and the reindeer on her sweater were bleached and cold down there in the hole. *Wait for me, Virginia, baby.* The lights behind me were gone again and I hit a slippery rise and stalled there, beating on the steering wheel with my fists and yelling, until I thought of the four-wheel drive gadget on the jeep, and I tore at the stubby levers until I had them set, the cold grease of the transmission fighting against me.

In four-wheel drive I got rolling again and instinct

and habit got me out of town and on the main road. Once I climbed out and walked along a gulley on the side of the road, squinting and feeling a tri-cornered rock marker with my frozen hands. My hands followed the shape of the landmark there, but I did not feel it against my skin, and I remember beating on it until the flesh popped away from the bone on the insides of my fingers. My mittens were gone. *Wait for me, baby.* My fingers were black in the glow from the headlights. It was dead night now. *Don't leave me, Virginia.*

The climb from the main road to the shaft was a soft, experienceless thing, all floating feathers of snow and now and then the wind sweeping a clean black strip against the sky so that the stars showed up there. Nothing hurt me physically, but the picture of her in the shaft on the bow of icy rock was burned into my sick brain, and the weak tears froze before they were shed. Perhaps I'd be in time with the rope. But what could I do with a rope? And what rope? It hit me in an almost smothering wave that I hadn't got the rope, that the shock of seeing Dooley had scared me off the thought of the rope. I was crawling now in the white blackness, the snow gentle and elbow-deep, the meat and bread in my right fist. *Are you hungry, Virginia? The gooseliver's very good tonight, madam, a specialty of the house. Eat it and vomit, madam. Vomit six hundred feet, madam. You won't bother a soul. Don't go away, Virginia.* I threw the meat and bread into the snow.

Chapter Fifteen

THE EMBERS OF THE FIRE winked in the bright
morning air on the edge of the shaft and the black circle of burned wood scraps shone in the sunlight, the
cinders clean and glinting as a blackbird's wing. I sat
there leaning toward the embers, and I remember
thinking it was funny someone should be laughing so
early in the morning and I kept looking around to see
who it was and I never was sure it was me. I figured it
might be somebody up in the rocks eating a prospector's breakfast, the way Virginia once told me the tourists did at Cripple Creek. It was more a cackling than
laughing. Virginia? Where the devil was Virginia? How
like a woman. Time for our morning swim and where
was she now? A half-dozen times I'd slogged down to
the old campsite and brushed the snow off the hollow
cooking rock. She wasn't anywhere around there, nowhere at all. She wasn't at the foot of the baby cliff where

we always slept.

I slapped my hands together and saw the snow fly off them in a thin puff of white, but I did not feel the slapping. How like a woman. Taking the Packard into town and leaving me out here on the edge of this strange hole in the ground. But she drove the Packard beauty-fully. She pasted the front-left fender onto the center-stripe like it was grooved on a rail. She'd take fine care of it and of the trailer, you could depend on that because no one could drive like Virginia. She was prob-ably getting herself a massage at Mamie's and when she came back to me she would tell me why she'd decided to leave me so long out here by the hole with-out anyone to talk to. I certainly wanted to talk to someone because she had been gone now ever since I could remember and she was nowhere around earlier when it stopped snowing and last night she'd been so busy bathing in the hundred-dollar bills she didn't know I was alive. And then she bathed in a pile of green canvas hats and Eddie came along and told her to give them back to him because he needed to get back to New Orleans and buy some bracelets for Loralee. I think that's what he said. He was dead drunk on bour-bon and Heavenly Hash and some of it was sticking in Loralee's hair but she didn't mind. She always felt fine. Lord, it was lonesome by the hole, so lonesome I crawled over now and then and looked in it, but it was just a deep red hole. On one wall, maybe forty feet down, maybe eighty or a hundred and twenty there was a lump, a kind of bow of rock sticking out, and aside from this there was absolutely nothing to see.

I was really glad to see Clell Dooley come strutting up the slope in the snow with Wayne Mackin and three or four other men, all of them wearing snowshoes and waving at me a long time before they got to me.

I tried to ask them if they had seen Virginia, but they didn't seem to know about her and they began hitting me and it seemed Dooley and one of the other men hit me a great many times before they took me off with them.

Now Available from Bruin Crimeworks...

James Hadley Chase

NO ORCHIDS FOR MISS BLANDISH
FLESH OF THE ORCHID

Fredric Brown

KNOCK THREE-ONE-TWO

David Dodge

DEATH AND TAXES
TO CATCH A THIEF
& *coming soon:* ***THE LONG ESCAPE***

Paul Bailey

DELIVER ME FROM EVA

Bruno Fischer

HOUSE OF FLESH

Elliott Chaze

BLACK WINGS HAS MY ANGEL

Visit the scene of the crime
@ *www.bruinbookstore.com*

CPSIA information can be obtained at www.ICGtesting.com
Printed in the USA
LVOW12s2152300114

371761LV00004B/264/P

9 780982 633977